The Billionaire's Love Child

A BWWM Pregnancy Romance By..

CJ HOWARD

Summary

On the surface, Billionaire Kevin has it all. He is rich beyond his wildest dreams and has the perfect trophy wife to go with it.

However, there is one thing he wants more then anything else in the world... A Child.

Only problem is, his wife refuses to give him any children and does not have any plans to do so ever. A divorce would be too messy for a man of his wealth so Kevin has no choice but to take drastic action.

He hires a surrogate with a twist.

He will father a baby with her but in this arrangement she will get to keep it. In return, mother and child will be supported financially for the rest of their lives. They will never need or want for anything.

For the beautiful and curvy Marina this is the ideal arrangement for her. She has always dreamed of being a mother but has never met a man worthy.

Kevin and Marina are about to embark on a very unique arrangement. One that promises to blur the line between love and convenience. Can such an arrangement exist without feelings getting involved? And can Kevin really stand by and watch his love child grow up without being involved directly?

Copyright Notice

Contents

Chapter 1

The warm California sun shone brightly on the massive white marble terrace, and it amplified the cobalt blue of the swimming pool and the intense green of the perfectly manicured gardens that gave way to the beach and shining sea behind the mansion. Kevin walked along the beach and gazed up at his enormous home. He wondered if his wife had risen for the day yet.

They had been sleeping in separate rooms for more than two years. Because she had been so affectionate before their wedding, he believed that their passion would endure through the years, but it had tapered off quickly and was now non-existent.

Ellen spent her days lounging by the pool, shopping and lunching with her girlfriends, relaxing at the spa, or not home at all. She would often leave on trips to other sunny beach resorts.

He had tried to stay close to her, but she had pushed him away and now it seemed like they were not much more than roommates in a giant home, empty except for the two of them and the house staff.

He looked out at the sea and sighed. With all the wealth and prosperity he had, he didn't really feel as though he had anyone to share his future with, and he truly believed that money wasn't the sum total of his worth. There was a hollowness in his heart, and even within his soul. He felt he was missing something, as if he were incomplete.

Kevin gazed at the sea and then turned and walked toward the house. When he entered the dining room from the back patio, he saw their housekeeper, Sarah, and paused to talk with her for a moment. Sarah was an older black woman, a bit on the heavy side, and three times as kind as she was big. She smiled up at Kevin.

"Good morning, sir. How are you today?"

.

"Good morning, Sarah. I'm alright. How are you doing?" he asked with a sincere smile.

"I'm fine, sir. Doing just fine." She nodded and watched him expectantly.

"Sarah, is Ellen up yet?" he asked with a twinge of anxiety.

She looked as though she was hiding her disapproval, but she showed no outward disrespect. "Yes, sir. She just woke up. She said she'll be taking brunch in her bedroom."

He nodded. "Thank you. Have a good morning." He smiled and then walked through the house and up the winding staircase to her bedroom. He knocked on the door and there was no response. He waited a few moments and then knocked again. "Ellen? Ellen, it's me," he said to the panel of thick wood before him.

There was still no response. He reached for the door handle and tried to turn it. It was locked. He had discovered shortly after she moved into her own room that she regularly locked her door to keep everyone out, including him. He knocked again and called out sharply to her. "Ellen! I'd like to talk with you, please open your door!"

After several long moments, the door was flung open, and standing in the doorway was a stunning woman with a look of absolute loathing and disdain frozen onto her face. She was just a little shorter than him, with large dark brown eyes, sharp high cheek bones, thin lips that had been inflated through surgery, and lightly tanned skin. Her long, sable brown hair hung down to her softly rounded hips and her surgically enhanced chest was visible through her sheer white negligee that reached from her shoulders to the floor at her feet. It hung slightly open and it stopped everything in his mind when he saw her.

She was stunning. His gaze drifted over her body to her face and then he looked into her ice cold eyes.

6

"What do you want?" she asked with irritation, glaring at him. "I was busy."

He took a deep breath and focused on the reason he was bothering her at ten in the morning. "We need to talk. I was hoping you had a few moments this morning."

She narrowed her thick lashes at him and considered it briefly. "What do you want to talk with me about?"

Kevin sighed. "Ellen, it is important to me, so it shouldn't matter what I want to talk with you about, we should just be able to have a conversation. May I come in, please?" he put his hand on her door and gave a slight little push.

"Don't be forceful!" she snapped at him. "I have things to do today, so make it fast." She turned and strode back into her room, her hips swaying from side to side as though she might have been dancing. She sat at her vanity and faced the mirror, reaching for the facial powder. "Well? What is it?" she asked with irritation.

He sighed and sat on the chaise lounge beside the windows a few feet away from her. "I keep thinking that it would be nice to have a family, Ellen. We used to talk about it all the time before we were married, and now here we are, all these years in, and there's no talk about it anymore, there's no effort to try, and hell, we don't even sleep in the same room or even the same bed. I feel like this house is so empty. I feel like we aren't going to leave any kind of legacy. What are we doing, Ellen? I want to leave a legacy. I want children."

She powdered her nose and picked up her lipstick, pulling it across her puffed lips and coloring them bright red. She pressed her lips together and pushed them out toward the mirror. "Darling, we aren't going to be able to have children."

He sat up and looked at her with surprise. "Why not?" He stood up and walked over to her, standing behind her and placing his hands on her shoulders, meeting her eyes in the mirror. "We could start a

7

family anytime, my love. Anytime at all. Let's do it! I want it so much. I want a family with you!"

She looked at him in the mirror with her dark eyes and then turned on her seat to face him. She ran her hands and sharp red polished nails up and down the length of his thighs. Kevin drew in his breath as he looked down into her beautiful face. She parted her lips, watching him intently, and stood up slowly, sliding her hands up his body, resting them finally on his solid chest.

He wrapped his arms around her waist and she leaned close to his mouth, locking her gaze with his and said softly, "Because I had a hysterectomy when I was eighteen years old… my love. You see, I don't want children. I've never wanted children." She tilted the corners of her mouth up in a tiny Cheshire cat sort of grin.

Kevin felt the blood in all of his upper body drain to his feet and his heart seemed to suspend its rapid beating and sit perfectly still in his chest. He blinked.

"What are you talking about?" he asked as shock and horror began to reverberate throughout him.

She pulled her sheer negligee open and revealed the sculpted body that was barely hidden beneath it. Kevin's eyes slipped down over her fully rounded and perky breasts, her narrow waist, curved hips and long slender legs. She looked like she had just stepped off of a magazine cover. She kept herself in flawless condition.

"Do you think I want some kid wrecking this beautiful body?" she said with a cold twist of her mouth. "I knew when I was sixteen that I was gorgeous, and I knew I didn't want anything screwing that up for me, so as soon as I turned eighteen, I had a hysterectomy and guaranteed that this body would always be mine."

She stepped close to him and pressed herself ever so lightly against him, her body barely touching his. "This body is what got your attention to begin with, isn't it?" she whispered. He was battling fury and desire simultaneously, and he raised his hand, his fingers

8

outstretched, and tentatively reached toward her breast, wanting to touch his fingertips to it.

She moved away from him quickly and his hand brushed at the air. He took a deep breath and refocused his mind and attention on her. "Ellen, you lied to me! How could you do that? We talked about having kids! How could you lie to me like that? You knew I wanted children right from the beginning, when we met!"

Ellen stepped over to her dresser and dropped her negligee to the floor, leaving it there and opening her drawers to pull out undergarments. She looked over her shoulder at him as she slowly slid on her thin designer panties.

"You talked about having children, and I let you talk about it. I never said I wanted them. I never said we should have them. I just let you talk and plan and I never said anything about it." She slung her long sable hair over her back as she turned to face him while she pulled her bra on. "You were so wrapped up in the idea that I just let you keep on talking about it. I had hoped that it was a phase you would eventually get over."

Kevin watched her in disbelief. "You let me go on about it and never said anything? You didn't think maybe I ought to know that the woman I was marrying couldn't have children when it was so obvious that I wanted them?" He felt as though he had been hit in the stomach with a wrecking ball.

She walked into her closet and turned on the light, and he followed her. She ran her hands over multitudes of hangers holding designer clothes specially made for her. "Ugh… I have nothing at all to wear. Look at this. I'll have to get some more clothes made."

She moved to another rack and flipped through the clothing there for a few moments before looking over her shoulder and scoffing at him. "Kevin, it's really not that big a deal. You need to get over it. After all," she said, pulling out a beautiful dress and shoving it back into the row of clothes as she continued looking, "you get to have me, and really, what could be better than that?" She pulled another hanger out and looked at the lovely pristine garment, contorted her face in disgust and threw it on the floor before going back to search again.

"What do you mean I have you? I don't have you! You're in your own room, you're always busy, and you never let me touch you anymore. It's been months since we made love. How do I have you? Ellen, I'm talking about having a family!"

She yanked another dress from the row and glanced briefly at it before scowling and tossing it on the floor. "Are you still going on about that? How can you still be talking about that? Oh my god! Look at this!" she began to yell and waved her hand at the large room they were standing in; all four walls featuring shoe racks, shelves filled with handbags, and rows of clothes handmade just for her.

"I have absolutely nothing at all to wear! You can't even take care of your own wife! How do you expect to be able to take care of kids? You're insane! I can't look at you anymore. I just can't. You have to leave. Leave now!" she said as she leaned over and scooped up one of her tiny designer dogs and stomped into her bedroom, plopping herself down on the giant bed where three other tiny dogs were lounging. He walked out of the closet and stared at her as she sat there on the edge of her bed, glaring at him. Her dogs began to growl at him.

"Forget about having children, Kevin, you would be a horrible father. I can't even imagine you destroying some kid's life by trying to be their parent. We are not having a family; we are both already busy living our own lives. What are you going to do, stop working long enough to try to raise a kid? Right."

She rolled her eyes and then angrily stared him down. "If you want kids, go have them on your own, and get out of my room! I can't believe you came in here and said all these awful things to me! Look how upset I am! My head hurts now! How could you treat me like this? You are wretched! Ugh! *Get out!*" She picked up one of the multitude of pillows on her bed and flung it at him, missing him by several feet, and her dogs began to bark loudly.

Kevin stood there for a moment, staring at the hypnotically beautiful woman before him who was ripping his heart out, and he felt his heart break under her feet. He turned quietly and walked out of her bedroom, closing the door behind him.

He walked down the hall and winding staircase to the main floor and headed toward the back of the house where his office was. It was more of a sanctuary for him by that point. He closed the dark mahogany door behind him and sighed deeply. He felt as though he had been blindfolded all through his courtship and marriage to Ellen. She was a beautiful, broken gift.

He looked around him at his office. The walls were covered in bookcases that reached to the ceiling and, on the far wall behind his massive dark wood desk with intricate carvings, there was a wall of windows that looked out onto a lush and beautiful garden with a koi pond and waterfall. He often worked in this room with the windows open so he could hear the relaxing sounds of the water and of the world living just outside.

Kevin sat at his desk and buried his head in his hands. How did he not know his wife was unable to have children? How had she hidden that from him? Did she really never talk about having children?

He thought back over their conversations and realized that she was right. She had never said a word about having children. How had he not realized that? Just minutes ago, she said that he wouldn't be a good father, and he pushed the comments from his mind. That couldn't be the case. Of course he would be a good father. He was kind and thoughtful, he had a good heart, a great deal of patience, a lifetime of wisdom to pass down… he was a billionaire; he certainly had the means to care for any children he might try to raise. He would be no worse than any other parent.

Her comments gnawed at him… *'If you want kids go have them on your own…'* he leaned back in his chair and folded his hands underneath his chin. Her words echoed through his mind and, as they twisted and turned, as they repeated over and over, they began to sink in and take hold.

 Her lie by omission… she could never have children, and she just let him believe otherwise… "Go have them on your own…" she had said. She had known right from the start just how important it was to him and she disregarded his need.

Kevin picked up his phone and thought for a moment before pressing his speed dial button. A male voice picked up the other end of the line.

"Yes, sir."

"Mac, could you please find out what it would take to locate a woman who is looking for a sperm donor?"

There was silence for a moment, then Mac replied, "Yes, sir. There are facilities that handle sperm donations. Should I get a list of facilities?"

"I'm actually thinking of locating a specific woman. I'd like to find one who is looking for a sperm donor, but one who would let me be part of the child's life as it grows. It seems that Ellen and I won't be having children together, and at her suggestion, I have decided to find someone else to bear a child of mine. I would provide the sperm, the woman would carry the child, I would pay for all of the child's expenses and upbringing and see the child whenever I like." The idea was still evolving in his mind, but even as it did so, he felt his heart growing excited.

Mac, Kevin's assistant, replied without judgment or surprise, as he always did, no matter the request. "Yes, sir. I'll look into it right away. Do you have any special requests?"

Kevin rubbed his finger over his chin. "Not really. Someone healthy, intelligent, responsible, hopefully attractive; things like that. I'm guessing someone like that who is looking for a sperm donor is probably looking for the same things I am."

"Yes, sir. I'll get right on that," Mac said, confidently.

"Thank you, Mac. I appreciate it. Oh… Mac, please don't say anything to anyone about this, and don't say anything to Ellen. I don't want her to know about it. She didn't want to be involved in procreation, so she doesn't need to know about this. It doesn't concern her at all."

"Yes, sir. Of course, I'll keep it to myself."

They hung up and Kevin sat there a moment and then picked up his phone again. This time he pressed a different speed dial number.

A man answered. "Hello?"

"Jacob, it's Kevin. How are you?" He smiled slightly. Jacob was an old friend of his, and also one of the best attorneys in California.

"Hey, Kevin, I'm great. How are you doing?"

"Well, some things have come up here this morning that I wondered if I might talk with you about," Kevin said, picking up a pen and turning it over in his hands.

"No problem. What can I do for you?" Jacob asked.

"Ellen just told me she isn't able to have children because she had a hysterectomy when she was eighteen, so I am interested in looking elsewhere to make that happen," Kevin began.

Jacob's shock came through the phone. "But I thought you two were trying for kids… how could you be trying if she knew she couldn't conceive? And what do you mean by looking elsewhere?"

13

Kevin sighed. "Well, my friend, I guess she lied to me. You're talking to a fool. She never wanted kids; she just didn't bother to tell me until now." He turned his chair and looked out the window into his garden. "She suggested I go have children on my own if I want them so badly, so I'm taking her advice.

"I have Mac looking for a woman who might fit this unique need. I'm hoping to find a woman looking for a sperm donor; someone I can have a child with outside of my marriage, without being unfaithful to my wife. The mother and child would be under my financial care and I could see the child whenever I want to, and Ellen would never need to know about it. It's the best fix for this broken situation, unless you have a better solution." Kevin sighed.

Jacob let a long breath out through his teeth. "Wow, Kev… that's a lot of risk. I don't have to ask how important this is to you; I know what it has always meant to you to have a family. Ellen's really pulled a fast one on you, my friend. I've got a lot of questions for you about this. First, how is your marriage to her looking?"

He took a deep breath and watched a bird splashing in the water at the top of the waterfall. "It's not what I want it to be, but I made a vow and I'm standing by that vow, Jacob. I don't want to lose my wife, and I don't want to be unfaithful to her, but I do want children, and, if I'm lucky, grandchildren one day."

"You're a good man, Kevin. A damn good man. Okay, next question, when you say 'under your financial care', what exactly do you have in mind? I'll need to make some changes for you."

"I mean that the procedure to accomplish the task, the full medical care, childbirth and ensuing living expenses for both the mother and the child until the child comes of age, and the child's education and lifestyle, are to be taken care of by me, without Ellen's knowledge." He was warming even more to the idea.

"Would you be changing your will and estate inheritance to include the child?" Jacob asked.

"The child would inherit everything, although Ellen would be guaranteed a residence of her choice and a generous monthly stipend for the remainder of her life, should I pass on before her." Kevin felt strongly about caring for his obligations and commitments.

Jacob was still absorbing the shock of the news. "Wow… that's… okay. Well, we'll start getting everything changed when you find your girl. You sound like you're really going to do this. Are you sure you want to? This is a massive and permanent undertaking."

Kevin thought for a moment. "I'm sure. Jacob, nothing is more important to me than having a family. You know that. I just wish Ellen had been honest about herself before we married. Thank you for this. I appreciate it."

"I'm glad to help you, old friend," Jacob said solemnly.

*

Two weeks later, Kevin was sitting in his office when Mac walked through the door. He had notified Kevin that he was coming, but Kevin was more than anxious to see him.

"There you are! Well? Where is this file?" he asked, half rising from his seat and then sitting back down as Mac hurried across the office and laid the file on his desk, then sat opposite him.

"I think we may have found just the right woman for you, sir. She is healthy, intelligent, emotionally stable and responsible. She is looking for a sperm donor because she wants to be a single parent." Mac sat at the edge of the seat, almost hovering, and looked at Kevin as he opened the file and started reading the paperwork.

Kevin reviewed her excellent medical history and her education and community work. He looked at her job history and residences. He looked at her family's history and then he turned the last page and saw the eight by ten glossy photos of her.

She was beautiful. Blue-gray eyes and dark mahogany skin, full sweet lips that curved into a genuinely happy smile, high rounded cheeks and something elegant about the way she carried and held herself. He stared at her images for a long moment, thinking about what his child might look like if born of this woman, and he liked it.

"What do you think, sir? Do you have any questions? I'm very familiar with the entire file and all of her information. I can answer anything about her for you." Mac was as anxious as Kevin had been before Mac gave him the file.

"I like her. I would like to meet her as soon as possible. When can we arrange that, Mac?" Kevin asked, leaning back in his chair and gazing happily at his assistant.

"She is in Santa Cruz. I can arrange a meeting tomorrow, or perhaps today, if I can reach her. She knows that there is someone interested in becoming a sperm donor for her, and she knows that the person is a private donor, but she doesn't know anything else. What works for you, sir?" Mac asked as he pulled out his phone.

"I want to meet her today, if we can do it," Kevin said, picking up her photograph and looking at her lovely face.

Mac was already on the phone. He spoke politely and professionally for a few moments and then hung up and looked at Kevin with a wide smile. "We can see her today, sir. She will meet us in Santa Cruz. I'll get the car ready."

Kevin called Jacob while Mac arranged for the car to come around and pick them up. Jacob said he definitely wanted to be there for the meeting and asked them to pick him up along the way, which Kevin agreed to. He could not stop the bubbling excitement growing inside of him.

Two hours later they were pulling up to the café where the woman said he would meet them. Mac decided he would stay with the car unless they notified him that they needed him, and Jacob and Kevin went inside the café.

They didn't see her when they went in and the barista looked at them sidelong for a moment and smiled. "Are you looking for Marina?" she asked.

Kevin smiled and nodded. "Yes, is she here, please?"

"She's at one of the tables outside. Come with me." The barista walked them to a shade covered round table, anchored securely beneath the sand on the beach. They sat, she took their orders, and then she disappeared. The woman was nowhere to be seen for a moment, but then Kevin saw her and tensed, and Jacob noticed.

"What is it?" he asked.

"It's her." Kevin watched her walking toward them. She was coming up the beach, her long curly hair tied back with a scarf which only partially tamed it from blowing in the breeze. Her sundress was hugging all of her body as the beach breeze curled and tugged it around her. She was smiling and wearing sunglasses that hid her eyes. She placed her hand on her forehead to shade her eyes, saw the men, and waved, heading toward them.

Kevin and Jacob both stood as she reached the table. "Hello, I'm Kevin and this is Jacob. You must be Marina," he said, holding out his hand. She looked at his hand and smiled widely, then leaned over to him and wrapped her arms around him, folding him into a hug.

He felt a little awkward at first, and then his nervousness seemed to thaw quickly, and he put his arms around her in return and hugged her back. He was amazed at how good it felt. She smiled at him and walked around the table to hug Jacob, who saw it coming and hugged her back right away.

She was shorter and very curvy, but not heavy. Her muscles were toned and strong, and her dark skin had a healthy glow to it, as did her wide and welcoming smile. Her spirit seemed to emanate a warmth like the sun, and everyone around her seemed to soak it in like they needed it.

"How are you gentlemen today?" she asked, sitting down and looking at them as she sipped her water.

They both nodded and smiled, saying that they were fine.

"Marina, it means a great deal to me that you could meet us here today. Thank you so much for that. I really appreciate it."

"I'm glad I could do it," she said with her happy smile.

"Well, if I may get right to it, the situation is this. I'm a married man, and I intend to stay that way for the rest of my life. I take my vows seriously; I love my wife, and I wish she and I could have a child, but it just isn't possible. I recently found out that my wife isn't able to have children, and it is very important to me to have a family to carry on my name and inherit what I have made for myself. It seems to me that the solution would be to have another woman carry my child and raise it as her own.

"Ideally, I want to be able to be part of the child's life and help raise it, to be there to spend time with it and to love it and care for it as a father should, but only as a father to the child, not as a husband to the mother, if that makes any sense.

"In return for this arrangement, I would glad to cover all medical costs associated with artificial insemination, maternity and pregnancy, childbirth, at which I would want to be present, and the entire expense of not only raising the child, but all the care of the household for the mother and child, as well as the education of the child through the college years. There would be no expense for the mother whatsoever, at any time."

Kevin finally stopped talking and took a breath, looking at Marina, who sat there and quietly watched him the entire time. She leaned back in her chair and smiled, stretching out just far enough to reach into the sunlight and let it shine on her for a moment, and then she sat back up and sipped her water.

"I'm sorry to hear that your wife can't have babies. That must be really hard for you both." She smiled at Kevin. She knew right away from the look in his eyes and the way that he spoke that she could trust him, and she liked him. She knew he was a good man. "How does your wife feel about someone else having your child?"

Kevin looked down for a quick moment and then raised his gaze back up to her. "Well, to be honest, she doesn't know, and I don't want her to know."

Marina tilted her head sideways and watched him. "Why is that, Kevin?" she asked curiously.

He knew he had to be honest with this woman if he wanted her to have his child raise it, and he already knew that this was exactly the woman he wanted for the job.

He sighed and leaned back in his chair. "I was led to believe that she could have children until very recently, when she told me she had a hysterectomy when she was eighteen. She made me believe that she could have children, and we dated and fell in love and got engaged and I married her, thinking that someday we would have a family.

"It isn't going to happen now, and that is something that she has known all along and never bothered to mention to me, knowing how important it is to me to have a family. Her priorities are shopping and spa days. My priority is having children. It would cause undue stress in our relationship to try to include her in this endeavor. It isn't important to her, and it is imperative to me. I hope you can understand that," he said sincerely.

She nodded slowly and her smile faded a little. "I wouldn't want to cause any problems in your marriage, but if you think it's best that she doesn't know about this, then I can do my part to make sure that doesn't happen, but… Kevin, do you really think that you can keep the fact that you have a child from your wife? How long do you think you can do that before she finds out about it? What would happen then?"

Marina leaned forward and Kevin caught a glimpse of the high curve of her breast and leaned back away from her to shield his view.

"She and I don't really speak much, or spend much time together. I honestly don't think she would find out because she has absolutely no interest in anything I do, but if she did find out, then I would help her cross that bridge when and if we ever got to it, but I would like to try to keep it clandestine for the time being, just to prevent any issues. Is that something that would be alright with you?" He looked at her hopefully.

She bit her lip and thought a moment, wondering how bad this man's marriage must be if he and his wife were so distant, but she realized that his need for a child was truly great and she liked the idea of his plan. She could have the child she wanted without having to be in a relationship. "How much of the child rearing do you want to be a part of?" she asked earnestly.

He smiled. It was the first real smile she had seen since he saw her walking toward him when she came to the table. "I want to be there for as much of it as I am able to be. Obviously, I couldn't be there every day, though I wish I could, but I would like to be involved as much as possible. I don't want to miss anything."

Marina nodded and smiled. "That sounds good. I like the plan you have. It fits well with my own goals."

He looked intently at her. "What are your goals? What would make a beautiful young woman like you want to have a child on her own without a husband? May I ask?"

She looked down for a moment and then looked back up at him. "I haven't been that lucky in love, to be honest. I was in love, yes I was. I loved that man with everything in me, and when he asked me to marry him and spend the rest of my life with him, I said yes, and I thought I was awake in a beautiful dream. But then my wedding day came and he left me at the altar, broken hearted and crying my eyes out.

"I wanted a family, too, Kevin, just like you, but those dreams were washed away with my tears when he left me there all alone.

"I'm focused on school and my career now, and I still want the family, but I decided that I don't need the man to go with it. I would rather save myself the heartache, thank you very much, so I'm looking for an opportunity to have myself a baby and raise it on my own.

"Your situation appeals to me; I think it would be fine to have you around being a father sometimes. I think I would like to share the responsibility without having to be in the relationship. It seems like the best of both worlds to me, to be honest. I'm also glad to know that you would be taking care of all the expenses.

"That's a huge relief to me, and something that I would really be grateful for. I wouldn't get that benefit going through a sperm bank. You seem like a good man, Kevin, and you want your baby for good reasons, like me," she said softly.

"Do you have any other questions for me?" he asked, leaving himself wide open.

"Not really. Not yet. I may later. Could I contact you anytime I need to?" she asked hesitantly.

"Yes, you could. I would hope that you would feel free to contact me anytime; you are certainly welcome to."

"Then I have no questions. I would be glad to be the mother of your child." She laughed at the silliness of her statement to this man she had just met, but she knew in her heart of hearts that it was the right choice and that nothing bad would come to her through him.

He stared at her for a moment, watching her blue-gray eyes, and her wide, warm smile, drinking her in, and then he nodded and leaned forward. "Okay, that sounds good to me. I'd like to be there for the obstetrician appointments, if that's alright with you. As I said, I want to be there for as much of it as I can be." He looked at her hopefully and she nodded.

"Of course. I'll let you know when those come up," she agreed.

Jacob pulled a thick stack of paperwork out of his briefcase and had them both sign two stacks worth of pages. There was one copy for each of them. They signed and sipped their coffees and made light conversation for a while, and after another half an hour, they were finished.

"Alright. I'll head in to the clinic today to make the necessary deposit, and your procedure will take place a few days after that. Apparently, it takes a few weeks for them to come back with the actual results to let us know whether or not the procedure was a success, so I will expect to hear from you and I will be in touch with the physician that we have chosen for this project. She's the best in the area. I have a good feeling about this." He stood up and leaned in to hug her, feeling much more natural about it this time.

She wrapped her arms around him, closed her eyes and hugged him back tightly. "I think this is going to work out really well." She released him, smiling up at him. She hugged Jacob goodbye and, as they were walking away, Kevin turned once to watch her as she strolled casually down the beach, her dress dancing around her in the wind, clinging to her curves, and her dark hair and skin shining in the sun. His heart felt warmer than it had in years, and he knew he had made the right decision.

Jacob thought the same thing and he said so. "You just did one of the smartest things I've ever seen you do, old friend. I'm so glad you did it."

Chapter 2

Kevin spent the next few weeks busying himself with his work and trying not to think about the procedure and how it had gone. He was working late in his office one night when there was a knock at the door. He looked up in surprise. He hadn't been expecting anyone. "Come in," he called out.

The door opened and Ellen stepped in, draped in a cobalt blue satin robe that clung to her body closely. Kevin's eyes drifted over her for a moment, and his breath caught as she walked toward him, her long sable hair hanging over one shoulder, her dark eyes looking at him like he was her prey, and her full red lips curved into a small smile.

He didn't fool himself into thinking she might be there for him, though it made him sad. "What can I do for you?" he asked carefully.

She walked around his desk and sat on the edge of it, facing him. He leaned back in his chair and she slowly lifted her left leg and placed her foot just inches from his crotch. Her robe fell away from her and he looked at her pale, bare skin as she maneuvered just enough that he could almost see what was under her robe.

She leaned forward and the top of her robe fell loose, giving him a generous view of her full bare breasts. "I just thought I would come see what you are doing. You've been busy lately and it made me think I should stop in and say hello," she said in a velvety voice. He could smell liquor on her breath.

"Hello, Ellen," he said, feeling nervous about why she was acting so seductively toward him.

"It's been so long since you kissed me…" she whispered, leaning toward him, taunting him. He stared at her and his heart began to pound. She was exceedingly beautiful and no matter how difficult things were between them, he wanted her. He always wanted her.

He looked up at her and she smiled down at him with her sultry lips and kissed the red painted tip of her finger, slowly, sensually, and then she lowered her hand and placed her fingertip on the inside of her left knee, which was inches from his face.

"Kiss me… here." Looking at her carefully, he turned his face slightly and pressed his lips to the place she had touched. Her smile widened. She moved her finger further up the inside of her thigh.

"Kiss me here, too," she said softly. He closed his eyes slowly and moved his mouth up the inside of her leg, leaving a gentle, warm kiss where she had touched her skin. She lifted her other leg and set her foot on the arm of his chair, pulling it closer to her, and she pulled her robe open so that her nude body was revealed to him and he drew in his breath.
"Kiss me… here." She touched herself lightly and then placed both of her hands on either side of his face, slipping her fingers through his hair until they were clenched behind his head, and she drew his face toward her core.

He gasped and felt his heart racing as he moved in toward her, slipping his hands under her thighs and around her hips, lifting her slightly and then closing his eyes and opening his mouth on her body. It had been so long since she had let him touch her, and the taste of her flooded him with desire.

The intimacy they were sharing had not happened between them in ages, and the intensity of it immediately ignited a white hot burning need in him. He held himself back and kissed her body tenderly at first, tasting the surface of her with his kisses, but then he began to flick his tongue over her and it took all his restraint not to delve deeply into her.

She lost her breath as he pleased her, moaning softly as he caressed her with his hot mouth. The sounds she made created an urgency in him that he could hardly hold back. He couldn't remember the last time she had let him interact so passionately with her. Kevin grew even hungrier for her, and he could no longer withhold his desire. He thrust his tongue into her, moving it about with abandon, drinking her in and gorging himself on the body he had ached for so long and so much.

Ellen gasped and cried out, clinging to his head and throwing her head backward in exquisite delight, until at last she climaxed and her whole body stiffened with her orgasm.

He groaned with his own need, and when she had relaxed from her pleasure, he stood quickly and began to unzip his pants, but she looked at him and held his hands in her own, pausing him for a moment. She leaned toward him, wrapping her legs around him and she placed her full red lips beside his ear.

"Kevin, baby, do you want me?" she whispered hotly.

He shuddered with desire and held her hands firmly, "More than you could comprehend."

"Well, baby, there's something I really need, and I want you to get it for me, would you get something for me?" she continued, running her tongue along his neck and the edge of his ear.

He closed his eyes and drew in his breath. "Anything. Whatever you need. Name it."

She pressed her soft warm lips to his ear and whispered again. "I need a brand new Lamborghini Reventon. A red one. I *need* it. Get one for me," she pleaded softly, her lips pressed lightly on his skin.

Kevin blinked a moment. "Of course, my love. You know I want to make you happy. Of course." His groin was solid and stiff, aching with need for her, and his heart was beating against his chest a mile a minute.

"Promise?" she asked, releasing his hands and slipping her hand down to massage the bulge at the front of his pants. "Get it today for me?" She pulled her head back and looked at him.

He closed his eyes as smoldering flames of desire burned through him and his breath caught. He ran his hands over her thighs to her hips and squeezed his fingers on her body.

"Yes, Ellen... yes... today..." he leaned forward to kiss her and she pressed her red tipped finger against his lips to stop him. He opened his eyes and looked at her.

She smiled her Cheshire cat smile at him. "Good. Let me know when it arrives and maybe if it gets here quickly, you and I can pick this little rendezvous up from where it left off." With that, she slid off the desk and straightened her robe, smiled again at him and touched her fingertip to his nose, then turned and walked out of the room, closing the door firmly behind her.

Kevin stared after her, panting, hard, aching, and frustrated. It was the click of the door closing that snapped him back to reality. He closed his eyes. She had used him. Again. He took a deep breath and walked carefully to the small refrigerator in the minibar set into the bookshelves of his library. He poured himself a strong drink and sipped it slowly as the fires of passion that burned in him began to die down to a dull roar and finally slip away like smoke from a doused blaze.

The days that followed his encounter with Ellen were torturous for Kevin. He focused heavily on his work, and true to his word, he had a Lamborghini ordered for Ellen, though it made him feel nauseous to do it. He was always a man of his word. The astounding price it cost him didn't bother him, it was the fact that she had used his desire for her to get it, and he had been left wanting her desperately, like an animal in a cage, starving.

One month after he and Jacob drove to Santa Cruz to meet Marina, Mac came into Kevin's office with a less than subtle grin and a thin file. "Sir! Sir… I have some news for you." He sounded as though he might burst with the news if he couldn't tell Kevin right away.

"What is it?" Kevin asked, taking the file from him and pausing to smile at the excitement on Mac's face.

Mac couldn't hold it in. His hand shot out toward Kevin and he grinned like an elf at Christmas. "You are going to be a father, sir, the tests just came back, and they are positive. Congratulations! Oh! I couldn't be happier for you, sir! Congratulations!" he repeated, grasping Kevin's hand and shaking it vigorously.

Kevin was in shock for a moment, absorbing the news. Marina was pregnant. It had worked… the procedure had worked and he was going to be a father. At long last, he would have a child; a legacy through which he could pass on his life's work and his enormous estate and wealth. He would have someone to love and raise, someone to cherish and lavish with all of his time and attention. Happiness welled up in him like a volcano of light, and it exploded in giant grins, tears on his cheeks, and a heart that pounded with joy.

He wrapped Mac in a quick embrace and then released him. "Thank you! Thank you so much, Mac! I couldn't have gotten it this far without you! I… wow… a father! I'm going to be a father! That's… wow… Fantastic! That's fantastic! Let's have a drink, Mac. Let's celebrate!" Kevin stepped quickly to the bar and poured them both a short nip of liquor, and they toasted Marina and the baby's good health, and Kevin's future as a dad.

"So how is she doing? Do we know anything? Do you have any information?" he asked, searching Mac's face excitedly.

Mac emptied his tumbler and sat down at Kevin's desk, opening the file, and Kevin sat across from him to look at it.

"She's definitely pregnant, and we know that it's one child. Sometimes in cases of in vitro fertilization, there may be more than one, but this time it is a single embryo. She is almost one month along, as she did the procedure right away for you. She's healthy and feeling well, no morning sickness or complications as yet. Her body is in excellent condition and she's very healthy and fit, so the doctor expects this to go, in her words, 'Like a textbook pregnancy.' So we have eight months to go and everything to look forward to. How are you feeling, sir?" Mac asked, concerned.

Kevin had to stop for a moment and gauge his feelings. He was elated beyond measure and there was a happiness in him that he had never known. It was as though his whole world and his whole life had suddenly opened up and wonderful possibility was his. He had no idea how to answer Mac.

"I'm so good that I've never been better. I don't know how else to describe it," he said with an ear to ear grin.

Mac grinned back. "Well, sir, when you are holding that child in your arms, I think perhaps the joy you have this morning may be topped, but until then, this is probably as good as it gets. I'm so pleased for you, sir, congratulations, again!" Mac beamed at him.

"You'll let me know when the appointments are scheduled? I don't want to miss any part of it."

Mac nodded. "Yes, sir. I'll make sure you get to each one of them."

"Great!" Kevin looked at the medical report in total bliss. He had a new life to look forward to and no end of excitement in waiting for it.

Chapter 3

Over the next few months, Kevin focused on his work and anticipated the arrival of his child. He was able to share his excitement with Jacob and Mac, and that was enough for him. Marina was in her fourth month before they went to a doctor's appointment together.

Kevin wasn't sure if he was more nervous or excited, but he had arranged to pick her up from her home to take her to the appointment. When they arrived, he stepped out of the car and looked up at the moderate little house. It was brightly colored in a warm yellow with white trim. He thought momentarily that the brightness of it reminded him of her personality, and it made him smile. He walked up the steps to the front porch where she was sitting in a comfortable looking rocking chair, enjoying herself.

He hadn't seen her since they'd met on the beach in Santa Cruz, and he felt refreshed just looking at her. Her long hair hung in big curls over her shoulder, and she was wearing a sundress that hugged the curves of her chest, but then drifted loosely from there down to just above her knees. She looked at him and smiled widely, then she stood and walked to him, wrapping her long dark arms around him in a welcoming hug.

Her hug was neither swift nor awkward, it lasted a long moment, as though she was truly glad to see him, and not only was he welcomed there with her, but he was cherished and appreciated.

Kevin was pleasantly surprised by it and he looked down at her when she released him, and paused, then said, "You know, no one has hugged me like that but my father, and he passed away the year I went to college. It's been quite a long time since then, and it's really very nice to be hugged like that. Thank you."

She tilted her head and her warmth shone through her smile at him. "It's my own personal rule that I don't let go first. I hug like I mean it until the other person lets go, then I let go, too. You never know how badly someone might need to be held." Her smile stayed on her beautiful face and her blue-gray eyes were alight with an inner peace and happiness that he found completely foreign and entirely fascinating.

She noticed him looking at her stomach and smoothed her hand down over her dress, holding it tightly to her. There was a slight swell beneath her hands. She smiled up at him. "Our little one is coming along. I think it takes after me. I'm never in a hurry; I just take my time and go along about my way. This one seems to be doing the same thing."

"I cannot imagine such an unhurried sort of lifestyle. It must be very relaxing… very peaceful," he said thoughtfully.

She nodded. "It is. I can't imagine living differently; I don't invite stress into my life. I get to the same places at the same time as everyone else, but I just go at a pleasant pace and enjoy everything around me as I go. It's much nicer that way."

He was silent a moment, watching her, just soaking her in, and then he lifted his elbow to offer it to her. "If you're ready, shall we go?" He was thinking to himself that she seemed like just the kind of down to earth, relaxed, happy kind of person that he would want to raise his child. He mentally thanked Mac for finding her.

They went to the appointment, and on the way she told him about how she had been feeling and how the pregnancy was coming along. She had a few bouts of morning sickness, but they had been few and far between and she recovered quickly. She discovered that she was sleeping more often, and she did notice that now, in her second trimester, she was feeling much stronger and healthier. She said she loved being pregnant and it suited her. He had to agree; she seemed to glow even more than she had when he met her, and that was saying something.

She watched him, watching her intently, and it brought her happiness and sadness together. He was incredibly handsome; he had soft brown hair that was carefully combed into a wave over his forehead, and it was cut short around the back and at the neck. He had dark brown eyes that seemed to go from mysterious and foreboding to sad and then to curious and happy, like clouds moving over the sun. His dark eyes were set into his clear fair skin and were framed by low brows and high cheekbones. He had a straight nose, a chiseled jaw and a soft smile.

He seemed to her to hold a wealth of secrets within him, and his face was a mask that he carefully operated so that nothing would be discerned about what was going on inside him, except what he wanted to be known. It made him very mysterious to her. She wondered what all of the secrets were behind his mask, and she knew that it would take a person a long time, maybe a lifetime, to unravel them.

Marina had agreed to be the mother to his child because she could tell right away that he was a good and honest man, that he was dedicated to anything he committed himself to, that he would love their child all of his days and do anything to care for and protect it, and that was of the utmost importance to her.

They arrived at the doctors and in no time, they were looking at a sonogram which showed them the tiny figure hiding within her belly. The moment the baby showed on the screen, they both fell in love with it. It became more real to them, as they looked upon it with their own eyes, as they listened to its soft watery heartbeat, and Kevin reached over to Marina, without thinking about it, and took her hand in his, holding it warmly, as they shared the moment together.

She glanced at him and saw his face aglow in the dark room, illuminated as it was by the light of the monitor. He looked like a child staring in wonder at something he couldn't quite believe, and it filled her heart with happiness to see him like that.

Her checkup showed that she was in excellent health and the doctor said she couldn't be more pleased. She asked them to return together the next month and hinted that she'd be able to determine the gender of the baby then, should they want to know. They delighted in the idea, and both of them agreed that they would want to find out what sex the baby was prior to its birth.

As they were walking out, Kevin offered his arm again, as was his habit for any woman walking with him, and she took it with a smile.

"You know, I was wondering if maybe you would like to go to lunch. I realize it's rather short notice, but if you're free, I'd like to take you out for a meal and then perhaps we could do some shopping for the baby together. I've discovered that I want to go purchase things for the baby, but I don't know what to get or what you might want, and it would be extremely helpful for me to have you there to show me what we ought to get for the baby." He looked at her hopefully.

She nodded. She'd been wondering how they would be handling the acquisition all of the baby furniture and products, and her questions were answered all at once. It was a relief.

"Sure! That sounds perfect. I'm free all afternoon. Thank you!"

He basked in the radiance of her simple happiness and pleasant ways, and he discovered very quickly that it relaxed him, and all of his tension seemed to dissipate. They ate at a little bistro not far from the baby store where they would begin shopping and he felt comfortable enough with her that he assuaged his curiosity about her personal life a little more.

"If you wouldn't mind, Marina, perhaps you could enlighten me a bit further about why you wanted to have a child on your own. I understand that you were left at the altar, but, would you mind telling me more about him? About what happened?" He didn't want to bring up sore subjects, but she seemed at ease about it when they had talked initially, and it was something he had made a mental note of, to question her further about it, just for his own knowledge.

She looked down at her hands in her lap for a moment and then looked back up into his dark eyes. She knew she could trust him and she saw no reason not to share her thoughts and feelings with this man. He was the father of her child after all, she reasoned.

"Kevin, I was so in love. I met that man when I was young and he romanced me, he made me promises, and he came after me like he couldn't live without me. He made himself a permanent fixture in my life; everywhere I went it seemed he was there waiting to talk to me, to watch everything I did, to be near me, to touch me. It was like I was the air he needed to breathe, and he just wouldn't live without me.

"I told him no and no again until he wore me down and made me laugh, made me love him, and I loved him with everything in me.

"He was my first love. He was my only love. He said he wanted me for the rest of my life, and he begged me on his knees to marry him, and I said yes, and my grandma cried when I told her, and we danced together in her kitchen. We planned our wedding and a few months later, we headed to the church and when I walked down that aisle, I didn't see him standing there.

"His brother came in to the chapel and walked partway up the aisle toward me, shook his head, and he said, 'He ain't comin', Marina, he ain't comin'. He's gone. You aren't going to see him again,' and I cried and cried. I thought I was going to die for a while.

"My grandma took me home and she worked on me for months after that, and I finally found myself again; I found my strength, and my own light. I found out who I was without him, which is something I never knew because I fell in love so young. You know, when you're young, you don't know who you are, even when you think you do… you don't, and by the time you go through something like that, you're changed again anyway.

"So I left Lamar in my past, and I focused on myself and my future. I graduated from high school, and I headed to college, and now I'm almost finished with school and I'm ready to start my own family; my own child and me."

33

She smiled at him. "You're just the right person to come along in my life, at just the right time; you're married already, you're a good man, and you don't want another woman. You don't want an affair, you just want a child and you can't have one.

"And me … I want a child on my own and I couldn't afford to have one on my own right now; there's no way. But you and I together? We actually make a really good pair. We're just right to fit each other's needs, and that's a blessing."

Kevin listened to her story and saw remnants of the pain she had been through, and it bothered him. He knew without a doubt that a woman as wonderful, as open and loving as this one was, should never have to feel pain that way, and it dug at him somewhere deeply that she had known that kind of suffering.

"Have you ever heard from Lamar? Do you know why he left or where he went?" he asked, feeling slightly uncomfortable about it.

She nodded. "He sent me a letter a few years later. He said he was devastated by what he had done, that he could never make his wrong right again. He wrote that he loved me still, but he was overtaken by fear of failing me, of never being good enough for me because he loved me so much. He hoped I had a good life. He said it was all he ever wanted for me."

"Do you believe him?" Kevin looked at her intently.

"I do. He may have left me there alone, and he may have hurt me worse than anyone else ever has, but he never was a liar," she said quietly.

Kevin stared at her and blinked. "Doesn't promising you that he is going to marry you and then not showing up make him a liar? He made a commitment and didn't see it through… he said he would marry you and he walked away from it. In my eyes, that makes him a liar." Kevin felt very strongly about keeping his word, and she could see that he was looking at it logically, where she was looking at it through the eyes of love betrayed.

She stared back at him. She had never considered the simple truth of it the way he had just stated it. Hearing those words said to her that way made all the veils of emotion that clouded her vision of it fall away. They were like thick fog blocking the sun, and they suddenly evaporated. Lamar had lied to her. Lied and left. She was astounded by the truth of it.

Kevin saw the changing emotions on her face and realized what he had done. It was an effect he had on many people when he spoke to them. He had a way of seeing things as they truly were, without filters. It suddenly made him feel as though he had stripped away some part of her naiveté; her innocent perspective of the whole thing, and it was disappointing to him.

"I'm sorry… I shouldn't have said that. I didn't mean anything by it. It's only my own opinion on something I know nothing about. Please don't pay any attention to it," he asked earnestly, but he knew that it was too late.

"No, Kevin, you have a solid point. You spoke truth, real truth, and truth can be seen when it's spoken; it's known, and I just didn't realize it before. I'm glad you said it. Don't feel bad about it. I'm in a different place in my life. He can't hurt me anymore. He hasn't hurt me for a long time. I let him go. You see, Kevin, we can't hold on to the things that cut away at us, or we wind up killing ourselves and those closest to us. The trick is to let the painful things go, and keep only the lesson."

She smiled at him, and her smile was still warm, but her eyes seemed a little different; perhaps a little older and wiser for the view he had shared with her, and he felt sorry for it.

After they ate, they went shopping and together they wound up purchasing all of the furniture for the baby's room, the car seat, the stroller, neutral colored clothing and diapers, mobiles, decorations, blankets, and no small amount of products for the baby.

They had a wonderful time, looking at everything and finding just the right things for their child. They talked about what their baby might be like and what they wanted for it in its life, finding that they were very similarly minded. It was nearly evening when he took her home. He walked her up to her door and she held his arm as they went.

"Now the challenge will be to get all of that furniture and everything put together. That's going to be fun!" she joked, rolling her eyes and laughing.

He stopped at the top stair with her and turned to look at her. The late afternoon sun was shining golden on her and it lit her up like a dream. He enjoyed the moment, gazing at her, and then he said, "Would you mind if I came over and helped you put it all together? I don't want to intrude, but if you could use the assistance, I would be very glad to give it a try." He was hopeful that she would say yes. He was thoroughly enjoying every aspect of the pregnancy, and he felt involved, which was important to him.

She nodded slowly and smiled. "Yeah, I wouldn't mind. That would be nice. Thank you, Kevin. I appreciate it. It's supposed to be delivered by next week, so maybe you could come by in two weeks and help me then. My schedule will be freed up a little more. Would that work?"

He smiled, delighted with her answer. "Yes, that would be fine. I'll be in touch and we can arrange the date and time. Thank you, it means a great deal to me to be included in as much of this experience as I can be."

Marina hugged him, and he waited to see if she would let go first, but she didn't, and what she had said was true; she didn't let go until he did. It was nice to be hugged as though he mattered, and when he stepped away from her and smiled at her once more before leaving, he could see in her eyes that he did matter, and it made a world of difference to him.

She watched him drive away from her front window and then went to make some tea, reflecting on the day she had shared with him. She smiled at the thought of his kindness and generosity; it was clear her baby would never need for anything, and she was really glad to discover that she and Kevin would probably be friends, which would make raising their child together a partnership. She hadn't really counted on that, and now here it was, and she could already tell that it would be a very good thing. Friends and partners in parenting. It was perfect.

Three weeks later, their schedules finally matched up, and Kevin knocked at Marina's door to help her put the baby furniture together and get the nursery set up. He was certain it wouldn't be any trouble at all, but he was surprised to discover that it wasn't as simple as it seemed from the directions.

She watched him work away at the crib for a while, which was the piece he had decided to tackle first, and after half an hour, she got down on the floor to help him.

"You don't mind if I try to lend you a hand, do you?" she asked with a big smile.
"Are you kidding? I need all the help I can get. Why didn't I have this delivered already put together?" he wondered as he unbuttoned his sleeves and rolled them up to his elbows.

"I'm afraid that the only thing that will be delivered all put together will be the baby," she teased, and he laughed with her.

They sat together and constructed the crib, the bassinet, the changing table, the mobile, the stroller, the dresser and the bookshelves and wall shelves. They hung the decorations and she made the bed in the crib. While he was working on the drawers for the dresser, she was bent over the crib, tucking the sheet in when she gasped and grabbed her stomach. Kevin was on his feet immediately, standing beside her. He placed a hand on her back as she turned to look at him, her blue-gray eyes wide and her mouth open slightly in shock.

"What is it?" he asked in a panic. "Are you alright? What happened?"

Before she could answer, Marina gasped again and clutched both hands to her stomach, then looked back up at Kevin and raised one hand to her mouth as tears filled her eyes and she began to laugh and cry simultaneously.

He stood confused for a moment, but she grasped his hands and placed them on her belly. At first, he was surprised, but then he realized what must be happening and his eyes widened, just as he felt a bump against his hand.

He laughed and grinned at her, and without thinking, pulled her into a strong hug. He held her tightly and they both laughed through their happy tears. He released her after a long moment and placed his hands on her shoulders, looking at her in utter amazement.

"Our baby! Our baby moved! Is that the first time?" he asked, his thoughts flying like lightening.

She nodded. "Yes! That's the first time I've felt our little one! I'm so glad you were here to share the moment with me! What a special experience! It's so incredible!" They both placed their hands on her belly and he looked at her in absolute joy as they waited for their baby to nudge them again. They didn't wait long. They got a few more bumps and they cried out in delight each time, thrilling at the miracle of life they had created together.

When it was evident that the baby was resting, Kevin lifted his hands to Marina's face and drew her near to him, resting his forehead against hers, smiling with her and calming their happy laughter. They held each other close for a moment and then he let her go and gently wiped tears of joy from her cheeks. She raised her fingertips to his face and did the same.

Their touches were soft and tender, and the air between them was warm. Their breath was stilled together for a long moment as they looked into each other's eyes, their fingers on each other's faces, and a powerful intimacy washed over them. They were silent, sharing their gaze, sharing the seed of a thought… the seed of curiosity… the seed of what if… and then they lowered their hands and smiled at each other widely, happy to have shared such a beautiful moment together.

"That was life altering," he said, shaking his head happily. "I've never experienced anything like it. Thank you for sharing it with me."

"I'm just so glad that you were here when it happened!" She turned back to making the crib up as he lowered himself to the floor to finished putting the drawers together. When they were done, he pushed the last drawer into the dresser and dusted his hands against his jeans.

"Well, it looks like the baby is all set in here. I guess you could probably get the rest; there's really not that much to do," he said, looking around at the nursery.

"Kevin," she smiled, "There's nothing left to do except bring the baby home. You've been incredible. Thank you so much for that." She smiled at him happily.

He nodded and looked away for a moment and then grinned back at her. "Well, I'm a dad now, so that's just part of the job. Hopefully, I will be putting toys together for Christmas and goodness knows what else. Tree houses and the like."

She just grinned at him. He looked at her for a long moment and then dusted his hands against his pants once more and said, "Well, I should probably be going." He smiled at her and she walked him to the front door.

"Let me know if you need anything else, alright? I'm anxious to help," he told her.

"I know. I'll get in touch with you if anything comes up." She leaned over to hug him once more. He held her more closely than he had before. They had shared a beautiful, wonderful, magical moment together and it had somehow bonded them a bit more than they had been already.

He let her go reluctantly and bid her goodnight before heading out the door. When it closed, she watched him go as she had before, and could not get the wide grin off of her face.

Kevin went with Marina to her fifth month appointment and they got to see the baby on the monitor again. The doctor told them they were having a daughter, and they hugged each other tightly in their exhilaration. They were both so thrilled with the news that it was all they talked about on the way back to her home where he dropped her off.

A few days later, when he could not get his daughter off of his mind, he texted Marina and asked her how she was doing. She answered that she and their daughter were fine. He asked her to send him a photo of the belly, and she promptly complied, sending him a text image of her growing round belly, and that prompted a phone call from him to her.

"Marina, what are we going to name our daughter?" he asked, his voice flooded with complete happiness.

"I don't know. I was thinking maybe we could name her after my grandmother, Madeline. Is there a name you'd like to use?" she asked him.

He was sitting in his chair, looking out of his office window. "My grandmother's name was Elizabeth. What if we used that as a middle name? Madeline Elizabeth? Do you like that?" he asked.

"Do you know what, I do!" she answered with a smile, "That has a pretty ring to it. That's a name that will get her nicknames, though. How do you feel about nicknames?"

He thought for a moment on it. "What if we called her by a nickname first? Then it would already be in place? We could call her Maddie."

Marina laughed and it sounded like sunshine and silver bells over the phone to him, and I it brought him comforting happiness. "You won't believe this," she said in her laughter, "that was my grandma's nickname."

"Is that alright? Should we do that?" he chuckled at the irony of his choice.

"Yes! I love it. I think that's perfect," she said softly. "How are you doing?" she added. She worried about him sometimes, sensing that he wasn't very happy in his life away from her.

He wasn't happy at home, but right at that moment, he could not be much happier, and he let that show through to her. "I'm perfect. I could only be better if our girl was here and I could hold her," he answered honestly.

"I'm glad to hear it," Marina replied, knowing that it was a truthful answer, but that it wasn't that good all of the time for him. She admired him for staying so dedicated to his word, and committed to a marriage that was so difficult. She had thought more than once that Kevin's wife was not only a lucky woman, but a bit undeserving of the man she probably didn't realize she had.

As the months went by and they saw the doctor more often, their anticipation grew stronger, and each day brought them closer to meeting their little girl and closer together as friends. They both had a strong admiration and attachment to one another, and though Kevin was visiting Marina once a week to help her prepare, to go to Lamaze classes, and to see their obstetrician, they still called and texted each other on days when they didn't see each other.

One week after her due date, Marina and Kevin were in frequent contact and neither of them was sleeping much, which was beginning to take its toll. Marina reminded him that Maddie was probably taking her time, just like her mom, and Kevin laughed at the idea. He had long since gotten used to Marina's way of not living a rushed life, and he found that he loved the relaxed feeling of that pace when he was with her.

He was snoozing lightly in his bed when his phone rang at eleven o'clock one night, and he bolted upright in bed and grappled with his cell phone for a moment until he got it answered. It was Marina, and all she could say was that her water had broken and it was time, before she gasped in pain and had to breathe her way through a contraction.

He told her he was on his way and hung up the phone. In moments, he was dressed and racing down the hallway toward the stairs when he almost ran into Ellen coming out of her room. She shut her bedroom door quickly and looked at him in alarm.

"Where are you going at this hour? What's the rush?" she glared. She was barely clothed in a sheer baby doll negligee, with nothing on underneath it. Kevin stopped abruptly and stared at her, then blinked and said, "I have an urgent matter I have to tend to. Good night, dear." Then he raced around her and down the stairs as she watched him go with a look of disdain upon her face.

He called Jacob and Mac on the way to Marina's house and within half an hour, he had her in his car and was arriving at the hospital. The emergency staff wheeled her into the maternity ward and he was stunned at their calm and unperturbed professionalism. He was amazed to think that they could be so held together while his entire world was changing right before him and his daughter was being born.

He said as much to Marina as he held her hand tightly, and she laughed at him in between her contractions. "Kevin, that's their job… it's what they do, every day, more than once a day, I bet." She smiled up at him. "Do you realize that's the first time I've been more logical than you?" She laughed again and then her body tightened in pain as another contraction gripped her.

"Breathe, Marina, breathe with me!" he urged, huffing and puffing right along with her as he encouraged her and held her hand. She breathed with him through the pain and then smiled tiredly at him. "You're a good partner and coach. You know that? Maddie is one lucky girl to have you as her dad."

He felt his heart swell and he touched his hand to her cheek, stroking his fingers over her face gently. "Thank you, Marina. You're going to be an amazing mother. I'm so glad I chose you. No one could be better." They shared a tender and heartfelt gaze for a long moment and then she cried out in pain with another contraction.

Kevin looked helplessly at one of the nurses. "Can't you give her something for this? Can she have an epidural? I can't stand to see her in pain like this!" He felt desperation for her every discomfort.

"Right away, sir, or she won't be able to have one at all. Her contractions are really close together now," the nurse answered. They brought in the anesthesiologist and he administered a shot that made Kevin go white as a ghost, but then a few minutes later, Marina was doing much better and he knew it had been worth it.

Jacob and Mac showed up and were able to check in with a fast hello before Marina and Kevin were told that it was time for Maddie to be born. The doctor positioned himself and Kevin stood beside Marina, holding tightly to her hand as she pushed with all her strength and might, over and over, until the doctor pulled their daughter from her mother's body, and Marina and Kevin were both crying at witnessing the amazing miracle that had taken place between them.

The doctor asked Kevin to cut the cord, which he did, and the nurses wiped their crying baby down and then handed her to her father, who wept at the sight of the beautiful tiny girl in his arms. He leaned down and placed her in Marina's arms, and then wrapped his arms around them both, for neither of them had known a more powerful moment in their lives, and neither of them could have withstood the full impact of emotion without the strength and support of the other.

Marina and Maddie were taken into their private room, and not long after that, Mac and Jacob were brought in to see the new mother and daughter. Jacob laughed good-naturedly when he saw Kevin holding his daughter.

"My friend, I've never seen a prouder father than you right now, right here," Jacob said. "Congratulations."

He shook Kevin's hand. Both men held the baby for a few minutes, although Mac had her in his arms a bit longer, and both of them fell in love with the little angel at first glance. She had her mother's dark curly hair and dark skin, and she had her blue-gray eyes, but it was obvious that she had her father's fine features and long graceful fingers.

They both had brought several gifts and spoiled the little girl on her very first day of life; it was something they both swore they would continue to do on a regular basis. They handed her back to her father and she looked at him with her little eyes as though she was trying to figure out where she was and who he was, and then she yawned and squeaked and fell asleep in his arms. Maddie had her father's entire heart, right from the first moment she was placed in his arms.

Kevin stayed with Marina for her duration in the hospital, and then took her and Maddie back to Marina's house, where they moved their daughter's bassinet into Marina's bedroom. It was the first time Kevin had ever seen Marina's bedroom, and he hadn't realized how simply she lived. She had only a box spring and mattress; no headboard or bedroom set, just a little wooden dresser against the wall. He felt suddenly ashamed, as though he had failed her somehow, though he didn't say anything.

He focused his attention on Maddie and Marina, and he did everything he could to help them and make their transition easier. Marina was exceptionally glad for his presence, wondering how it would have been to have faced the monumental experience of childbirth and the aftermath on her own with no father around, as she had originally planned to do. It seemed like another lifetime ago to her, and she was grateful for him.

Kevin sat on the bed with Marina and watched her nurse their daughter until the baby slept, and then he helped Marina stand up and they set the little one in her bassinet. He bit his lip trying to hold in the emotions that cascaded through him, but Marina saw his face and looked up into his eyes.

"What is it?" she asked, concern in her voice.

He shook his head and tears spilled down his cheeks. "I'm overwhelmed. I… I'm just overwhelmed. This is such an incredible gift. I thought I was a wealthy man until today, but now I know what true wealth is.

"Looking at her, and at you," he whispered, lifting his hand to her cheek and cupping her face, "I know there's nothing else in this world that I could ever really ask for, other than health and safety for the two of you." He moved his thumb over her cheek and she placed her hand on his and closed her eyes.

"I feel that same way, Kevin. We are so lucky to have what we do." She turned her cheek slightly and kissed his palm. His heart began to pound and hers matched his beat for beat, as she opened her eyes and looked up into his. Their breath mingled and their eyes were locked together as they held each other close. He leaned forward and their parted lips were a moment away from each other, but he turned her head in his hand and kissed her cheek. She closed her eyes tightly and closed her mouth, breathing in deeply through her nose and then releasing the breath slowly.

"I'd better go." He said in a whisper against her cheek. Then he pulled his head back from hers. "Please call me if you need anything at all. I'll be back later to help you again." He let his hands fall away from her and he took a step backward and drew a deep breath. She smiled at him and slowly walked with him to the front door.

He hugged her carefully and thanked her again for their beautiful daughter and all her hard work, and then he walked out the door and she closed it behind him and turned, leaning her back against it, and shut her eyes tightly.

"Don't fall in love with a married man. Don't fall in love with a married man," she whispered aloud to herself. "That's my new mantra. Don't fall in love with a married man. It can't be love. It's hormones," she reasoned with herself. "I'm filled with an ocean of hormones. I'm not going to fall in love with a married man." She repeated it to herself as she walked back down the hall to her bedroom and her sleeping baby.

Kevin got into his car and placed both his hands on the steering wheel, then lowered his forehead to rest on his hands. He told his phone to call Jacob, and in moments, Jacob was on the line as Kevin drove home.

"How's it going for the new dad?" Jacob asked with an obvious grin.

Kevin sighed deeply and there was a long silence on his end.

"Kev? Buddy? You there?" Jacob asked with slight concern.

"I'm here," Kevin answered quietly.

"What's up, Kevin? You don't sound like the ecstatic man I left at the hospital. Is everything alright? Marina and Maddie are okay?" Concern was growing in his voice.

"They're both just fine, thankfully." Kevin spoke in a low tone.

"Then what's bothering you? You never sound like this unless you've had another fight with Ellen. Is it Ellen?" Jacob continued.

"In a way, it kind of relates to her." Kevin sighed. "Jacob, I have had a little problem that has just become a big problem."

"What's that?" Jacob asked, patient as ever.

"I think I'm falling in love with Marina." He finally spoke the words aloud. He had wondered. He had denied. He had considered and ignored and pretended otherwise, but now he could not turn away from the fact that she was the only woman on his mind and in his heart, and she was what he wanted more than anything.

Jacob did not sound surprised at all. "Yeah, buddy, you are. So, are you just figuring this out?"

Kevin was astounded. "You knew?"

Jacob laughed at him, though lightly. "Yeah, well, it was pretty apparent about halfway through Marina's pregnancy, and Mac and I saw it right away. Matter of fact, I think I won the bet on this one."

"The bet?!" Kevin was even more surprised, though somewhere in the back of his mind he realized that he shouldn't be.

"The bet. See, Mac was sure you would admit it before Maddie was born, and I said you wouldn't admit it until after she was born. So, I won. How are you feeling?"

"Confused, and not confused," Kevin said quietly, his tone filled with sadness. "I know what I want, but I'm already committed. I can't have what I want; at least, not all of it. I can be Maddie's father, and I can be Marina's friend and partner."

"But not her lover. Not her husband. I know. Listen, Kevin, I realize this may come as a surprise to you, but you could get divorced. I could have that handled for you pretty quickly, actually." Jacob sounded sympathetic.

"I can't do that, Jake, I am married and I made a commitment to my wife, who is at our home right now under the impression that her husband is away on some urgent business. It's bad enough I was indirect with her, without considering the fact that I've fallen in love with another woman who just happened to have my child, and who she knows nothing about. Husband of the year, here. I cannot, I will

47

not, break the marriage vows I made to my wife. I swore to honor and love her until we died."

Jacob sighed loudly. "Kevin, you might be the only man on the planet who actually took that vow as seriously as you take that vow. If you keep talking like that, you're headed straight for a mid-life crisis, and you're still twenty years from that. Calm down. Listen to me.

"I understand your dedication to Ellen. I do. But I want you to do this for me. Take a good solid look at your marriage and really think hard about why it is that the two of you are together, and what good you are bringing to each other by being in each other's lives. Then, after you've had time to give it a lot of consideration, call me and I will draw up your divorce papers."

"It's not going to happen, Jacob. I'm just going to have to suffer through this and try to hold back the feelings I have for Marina. I will not break my wedding vows. Hopefully, time will make it easier." Kevin sighed and rubbed his temple. He was exhausted from the duration he had been awake bringing his daughter into the world, and from the emotion that was flooding through him. He pulled into his driveway and continued his call on the cell as he walked toward the house.

"Are all of the papers drawn up for the girls?" he asked, referring to Marina and Maddie being put into his will and set up for monthly stipends.

"It's all done, buddy. Get some rest. I'll talk to you soon," Jacob said kindly. "And Kev... just so you know, there's a much needed ending and a very happy beginning just waiting for you anytime you're ready. It's just a signature away my friend. Congrats on your beautiful baby girl."

"Thank you, Jacob. You're the rock I couldn't live without. I appreciate you, buddy." Kevin suppressed a yawn and closed his front door behind him. He hung up and took one step, and then something flew past his head and smashed loudly against the wall next to him, and shards of porcelain flew all around him.

*

He jumped aside and looked around as adrenaline rocketed through him. Ellen was flying down the rounded staircase at him and he could see that the object in pieces around his feet had once been the Ming vase that stood proudly in the hollowed shelf on the wall of the stairwell. He knew he was lucky she was a terrible shot; she didn't miss hitting him on purpose.

"What in the world are you doing?" he asked, his voice raised.

She flew at him and shrieked. "You! You *bastard*! How could you?! All this time, all these months, and *I just found out*! You *liar*! You *selfish*," she reached him and pounded both her clenched fists against his chest, "*horrible*," she pounded him again, "*bastard*! How *dare you*! How dare you do this to me!

"I am your *wife*! I'm supposed to be the *most important person in your whole life*! You *son of a bitch*!" She was screaming so loudly now that he had to turn his face slightly from hers, as he held her shoulders firmly, keeping her at arm's length from him to reduce the amount of physical damage she could do to him.

His heart sank. He had no idea how she found out about Marina and Maddie, but he would have to try to explain to his wife as best he could how he had secretly had a child with another woman behind her back without cheating on her. It seemed like the biggest lie and paradox of his entire life. Guilt washed over him and he hung his head.

"Ellen, I can't even think of where to begin or how to explain. I'm so sorry; I'm sorry to have kept it from you, I'm sorry to have done it without you knowing, and I'm sorry that you found out the way you did." He began with apologies, as remorse was his greatest emotion just then, and he did want to try to appease her justified anger with him. She had every right to be furious.

"You better start apologizing, you *rat bastard*! You're the sorriest man I ever saw!" she pulled herself from his grasp and began to pace in front of him, her red silk robe swirling like a bloody cloud around her body. "What in the hell made you think you could get away with it? Did you think that just because you went behind my back and did it anyway that I wouldn't be able to do anything about it when I found out? Is that what you thought? What the hell is the matter with you?"

He sunk into the sofa in their sitting room and she stalked around him like a lioness about to attack her prey. "How stupid do you think I am? You must think that just because we're married that you can get away with anything you want." She stopped in front of him and leaned over, pointing her sharp red nail directly into his tired face. "Well let me tell you something, you lying jerk, you're going to send that piece of junk back and get me the one I asked you for to begin with! How dare you try to pass that crap off on me!" she hollered at him.

He blinked and looked up at her. "What?" he asked stupidly.

She began to pace again. "There I was, so happy that you said you would buy me the Lamborghini that I asked you for; a vehicle that I have earned merely from the duress of being your loving and devoted wife for so damn long! And you led me down the primrose path, lying to me, making me believe for all of these months that you were providing me with what I asked you for, what I needed, and then what do I find in the driveway today? Is it my Reventon? Is it what I asked you for? *No*! No, it's not.

"All these months, you filthy liar, all these months I've waited and what's sitting out there for me today? An Aventador. That's right, an Aventador. Is it too much to hope that I could get a little *appreciation* from you? Some honesty? That you could give your loving wife what she asks for instead of what you think she ought to have? What kind of cold, heartless, selfish bastard are you?" She twirled as her pace hit its stride and she stomped back to him and pulled open the red robe, revealing her fully nude body.

"You're going to be a lonely one, Kevin, because you aren't touching this body again for a very long time. In fact, you won't even be seeing it again until my car, the right car, is sitting in the driveway, just like you promised me it would be." She snapped her arms closed around her, drawing her robe tightly about her body. "*Bastard*!" she snapped at him and then turned and stalked back up the stairs.

Kevin sat there on the sofa in absolute shock. He hadn't realized his mistake in buying the wrong car for his wife. He was certain that she had found out about Marina and Maddie and was ready to kill him for having a child out of wedlock with another woman.

He was stunned that she was so infuriated about a vehicle. He looked up at the empty stairs where she had disappeared and shook his head in wonder at her. What had she become? When did something like a car become so important to her? Her threat of withholding herself from him seemed irrelevant to him, as firstly, she regularly stayed away from him anyway; in fact, he couldn't recall the last time he had made love to her, and secondly, he no longer wanted to.

What he wanted was the beautiful dark woman lying in her bed beside their newborn daughter.

He picked up his phone and called Mac.

"Yes, sir! Congratulations again on your beautiful little girl, sir, she's just perfect!" Mac could not hide his utter delight and joy.

"Thank you, Mac." Kevin said with the first smile he'd had since he left Marina's house. "I want you to find a really stunning wood bedroom set, the nicest that you can, and have it delivered… uh… already assembled or have the delivery guys assemble it, to Marina's place. Also, send her a dining room table and a new living room set. Something beautiful and comfortable. She likes natural looking wood. Send it right away, but make sure to arrange a good delivery time; she needs her rest."

Mac was only too glad to do it. "Yes, of course, sir. Right away. Is there anything else?"

"I guess so, Mac. Ellen is a bit put out that her Lamborghini is an Aventador, rather than the Reventon she'd had her heart set on. Would you please see to exchanging those for her? It's a little more than I am able to deal with today. Thank you, Mac. You're a godsend."

"Immediately, sir. No problem. If I may, sir, get some rest. You sound exhausted." Mac's tone was filled with sympathy and concern.

"That I am, Mac, that I am." He sighed and hung up, then headed for his bedroom and passed out almost at the moment he placed his head on the pillow. He was so tired that he did not even dream, but when he woke, it was the next day, and when he was awake enough to remember and realize that he was a father, his only thoughts were of Marina and Maddie, and after a quick shower and a change of clothes, he was out the door to see them again. Nothing could have kept him away.

He had been given a key to Marina's house during her last months of pregnancy, and he used it when he came in to see them. Marina heard the door and her heart leaped as she called out to him, happiness filling her and overwhelming her.

"We're in here!" her voice floated down the long hall to him.

He grinned when he heard her, and everything in him came to life. He hurried down the hall and stepped through her bedroom door. The room seemed much smaller to him, but that was because it was filled with a truly incredible new bedroom set, and there on the new carved wooden canopy bed, was his daughter and her mother.

Kevin stepped up to the side of the bed opposite Marina, and climbed onto it next to her. "Hello there," he said with a grin he could not hold back. He leaned over and kissed her cheek and she closed her eyes as he lingered near her for the briefest of moments.

"Hello, Kevin," she said and smiled. She looked down at the tiny girl in her arms, the one nursing at her bared breast and said softly, "Look who's here to see you! Your daddy is right here, honey! As soon as your tummy is full, we'll let him burp you, okay?" she cooed with happiness.

Kevin laughed. "This is going to be interesting! I'm glad to do it, though. I'll burp her and you can eat the Chinese food I brought. It's organic; I had it made especially for you. You need to keep up your healthy diet. You're still eating for two people." He grinned, touching Maddie lightly on the forehead as she suckled away at her mother.

"I'm so glad to be here." He sighed and leaned against the pile of pillows behind them, looking up at Marina. "There is no one in the world that makes me feel as relaxed and happy as you do. I'm grateful for it. You should know that." He said it softly, his gaze holding hers.

She smiled gently at him. "I know that, Kevin. You do me just as much good, too. Never doubt that." There was an unspoken understanding shared in their look, and then she broke the visual connection and her eyes went back to the girl in her arms. "So what kind of Chinese did you bring?" she asked. "I'm so hungry!"

"I'm not sure… something with cashews, vegetables and chicken," he said with a sly smile.

"I love that!" she said happily.

"I know," he replied quietly to her. He pulled plates out of the bag he had carried in and made a dish for her. She finished feeding Maddie and as she handed her to Kevin, he had to pull his eyes away from their magnetic gaze at Marina's bare breast. There was something strange and beautiful to him about the two different emotions he felt; one of tenderness and adoration at seeing her nurse their child, and in which there was absolutely no sexual attraction.

But when his daughter wasn't at her mother's bare breast, there was unquestionably a sensual desire that swelled in him. He closed his eyes and turned his head, marveling at the wonder of womanhood, and wishing desperately that he could look at Marina as a friend again, trying to remember if he ever really had looked at her in a completely platonic light.

Marina covered herself and took a dish of Chinese food, diving into it while laughing and instructing Kevin to place the burp cloth over his chest and lay the baby on it while he patted her back. He was delighted to be so close to them both, and to be involved in the care of his daughter on such an intimate level.

He hadn't expected it. He had assumed that he would be there regularly, but he never realized how much love he could feel for his child, or how much he would need to be around her. It was an insatiable need for him, as imperative as breathing, and he neither could, nor wanted, to deny himself the pleasure of it.

"Thank you for the furniture." Marina said quietly, waving her hand at the mass of wood around them and the fine light linen canopy stretched out above them. "I love it. It's exactly what I would have chosen if I had been shopping for it. All of it. The living room, the dining room, and in here… Kevin, you really didn't have to do that for me. I was fine with what I had, but I want you to know how much it means to me that you sent me all of this. It's a tremendous gift and I really appreciate it. You've done so much for me. Thank you," she said, ending with a quiet thanks as she tried to keep her emotions in check.

He shook his head. The stark contrast between Ellen's fury and violence over having gotten the wrong model Lamborghini and Marina's humble gratitude at having received furniture from him was nothing short of polar opposite.

"I'm sorry I didn't let you choose what you wanted, but, when we came home… uh… when you came home yesterday, I didn't realize that you didn't already have something like this, and I wanted to get you a gift for Maddie's birth. Just a little thank you gift, and I wanted you to have it right away, so there wasn't really time to shop for options," he said almost awkwardly. "I'm really glad you like it. I tried to pay attention to what you liked when we were shopping for Maddie, and I'm just lucky I listened."

"You got it exactly right." She leaned her head back against the pillows and smiled at him. "If I had all the furniture in the world to choose from, this is what I would have chosen. Thank you so much," she said, turning to kiss his cheek. Then she lingered there, the scent and feel of his skin on her lips holding her like a strong tether. She drew in a breath and pulled herself back to where she was resting.

"Well," she said, making her voice lighter. "Has she burped yet?"

Kevin dragged himself back to reality and left the sweet moment which gave him pause when her lips touched his cheek, and he imagined kissing her lips; tasting her and breathing her in.

"Burped? Um… no. She fell asleep." He took a long, slow deep breath and focused on the way his life would continue to be. He rubbed Maddie's back and kissed the top of her head. She smelled sweet and clean, and he inhaled her scent and locked the perfection of it away in his heart forever, so that he could close his eyes at any time and bring himself back to this moment with her.

Marina finished her Chinese food and looked at Kevin. "Do you want me to hold her while you eat?"

He shook his head slightly. "No, I'm just going to hold her here next to my heart for a while. My heart is hungrier than my body at the moment."

She stood up from the bed and picked up the bag of food. "Then I'll put this in the kitchen for you and you can enjoy it when you are ready."

As Marina left, he watched her disappear, her long curls pulled up into a pile at the back of her head, her white cotton nightgown flowing out behind her. Kevin whispered to his daughter, "Maddie, I love you so much, my girl, and I love your mother, too, much more than either one of you will ever know." He kissed her soft head again and then watched her sleeping, mesmerized by her loveliness.

When Marina entered the room again, she had two cups of hot tea in her hands, and she set them on the new bedside tables, one beside Kevin, and her cup on her side of the bed, then she climbed in next to Kevin and snuggled up to him. He looked down at her and she smiled up at him. He lifted his arm and she moved closer to him, laying against him, her head on his shoulder, her hand on Maddie's back, as his arm closed around her and drew her near to him.

Marina closed her eyes and wished with all of her heart that it could be that way between them every day, that Kevin didn't need to leave, that he had no wife to go home to, and more than all of that, she wished she hadn't fallen in love with a married man, for indeed she had, mantras be damned, fallen head over heels in love with this beautiful, kind, dedicated, honest, loving, genuine, incredible man, who held her and their daughter in his embrace.

All she could console herself with were the beautiful moments that they shared, and the knowledge that he would always be there for her in this close friendly capacity as a partner and father, and she told herself that it would have to be enough. She couldn't ask for more than this. It was just going to have to be enough.

They fell asleep together, the little family, and later in the evening, Maddie woke them with her soft newborn cries. They changed her diaper and talked to her, soothing her, and Kevin watched in adoration as Marina fed her daughter and rocked her back to sleep. They placed her in her bassinet and stood side by side looking down at the best blessing of their lives.

"It's time for me to go," Kevin said quietly, hating to say it and wishing desperately that he could stay in this cocoon of bliss he had made with the woman beside him.

"I know."

.

He turned to her and pulled her into his arms, holding her closely to him, and he didn't let her go for a long, long while, so as her rule applied, it was him that eventually let go of her, and she looked away from him as he leaned down and kissed her cheek lightly, then turned and walked to the door. She climbed back into bed and pressed her head into the pillow, her back to the place where he had laid, her face toward the bassinet holding her baby. She did not look at Kevin.

He looked at her, lying there, and wished with everything in him that he could go to her and hold her, that he could kiss her lips and touch her, making love with her in that bed. Then he let the wish go, like a balloon on a sunny day, and it drifted away from him as he turned and closed the door behind him.

It was a long drive home, and it seemed to him that all of his drives home had become longer and longer, each time he drove them, but none so long as the two days since his daughter had been home.

He could not stop the myriad of thoughts and memories running through his mind. He felt as though he was being ripped apart; clinging steadfast to his ideals and morals on one hand, and wishing with everything in his soul that he could be with his baby and her mother for the rest of his life on the other hand.

He thought about what Jacob had said about finding the mutual value of his marriage and he pushed the thoughts from his mind. It didn't matter what value his marriage was, what mattered was that he had made a commitment and he must stick to it, or else what was his word worth?

He pulled into the drive and turned off his car. He rubbed his hand over his eyes and after a deep sigh, stepped from the vehicle and walked into the house. It was just past dinner time, and he expected that Ellen would probably be in the dining room. He had no wish to see her just then, so he walked up the winding staircase and was just passing her room to get to his when he heard her, and he recognized the sounds she was making. What he didn't recognize was the male voice in the room with her.

He reached for her bedroom door handle and twisted it, amazed that it was unlocked, and he pushed it open. Shock and horror hit him like a solid wall, knocking the wind out of him as his eyes fell upon the scene in Ellen's bedroom.

There upon her bed was one of their temporary gardeners, Enrique, tanned and toned, young and rippled with muscles. He was laying nude on Ellen's bed, and Ellen, fully nude, sat astride him, her hands planted in the satin sheets at his shoulders, as his hands were clasped firmly over her breasts, one of which was partially covered by his wide open mouth. Her knees were spread far apart and she was moving wildly over his hips, grinding away passionately, moaning loudly in pleasure as she flipped her long sable hair over her back and cried out his name.

They hadn't even noticed that Kevin had come in the room. They just continued on in their impassioned coupling, as he stood there almost in a trance, watching his wife screw the young man who had been around lately to fertilize the great lawn. Kevin could not move from the spot he was standing in, and he could not look away. He was completely dumbfounded.

"Oh!" she cried out loudly, "Enrique! Yes!" She bent down over his face and he released her breast from his mouth, so that she could kiss him. She planted her red lips on his and kissed him ardently as his hands moved to her hips and he grasped her buttocks tightly in his hands and rammed himself solidly into her, over and over as she cried out in delight.

Somehow, Kevin found the will to move himself, and he stepped toward them.

"Ellen," he tried to say, but no sound came from him. He felt as though he was in some horrible, wicked dream; some nightmare in which he was present but no one could detect him. He lifted his hand slightly toward her as she rode Enrique harder and faster, her cries building in volume and intensity.

"Ellen!" he called out again, and some rasp of a sound emitted from his throat. She cried out as her orgasm came over her fully, and she arched her back as Enrique clamped her hips down onto his own and growled at her and shoved himself completely into her, reaching his own orgasm and gasping as he climaxed inside her, and as her moans began to subside softly.

"ELLEN!" Kevin managed to yell out. They both heard him then, and they both jerked their heads up to look at him in shock as he took a few more steps toward them. He felt with each step as though he was impaling himself upon a poisoned blade.

Tears were running down his cheeks as he watched his wife's face change from shock to absolute fury. Enrique had the decency to look horrified and slightly ashamed, but Ellen, who slid herself slowly off of the erection that was stuck deeply inside her, rolled off of the bed with an angry scowl that burned Kevin right to his soul.

"What in the *hell* are you doing in here?" she screamed at him. "I demand an answer! I didn't invite you in here! You think you can just barge right into my room whenever you want to? Now look what you've made me do!" she shrieked, waving her hand behind her at Enrique, who was scurrying off of the bed and searching for his clothes that were scattered haphazardly across the huge room.

"You wouldn't get me the car I needed, and that meant that I had to be left all alone, that meant that I had to go without any love, without any affection at all, and your neglect subjected me to so much loneliness that I couldn't bear it! What kind of a lousy husband are you, anyway? Never touching me, never wanting me, always working… you're married to your job!

"You take off from the house in the middle of the night going god knows where to do god knows what, and here I am, all alone, day in, day out, while you're busy with everything else but your own wife, and now look what I've had to resort to! Letting this filthy yard man have his way with me, because you weren't around to protect me, to love me and want me, to fulfill your husbandly duties to me! How could you leave me all alone like that! Look what your neglect has made me do! Look what I've been reduced to! Scrounging for love like a beggar!

"I've had to search for someone, anyone at all who would make me feel like I was worth anything at all, because you made me feel worthless! Treating me with so much disregard the way you always do! You're despicable! You have the unmitigated gall to call yourself my husband? What husband leaves his wife to wilt away like some flower on a forgotten windowsill? You're such a hateful bastard! This is all your fault! Totally your fault! I never would have had to sink so low as to let this garbage touch my pristine body if you weren't always ignoring me! If you weren't always gone! You cold hearted selfish bastard! If you had only given me the car I asked you for to begin with, none of this ever would have happened!

"But all you can think of is yourself, all you care about is yourself, and you never give me a single thought, not even a moment! I've been so isolated! So alone! There was nothing else I could do!"

She yelled at him and wailed bitterly as she stood there before him, nude, the gardener's semen running down her thighs, as he found the last of his clothes and vanished.

Kevin looked at her and raised his chin slightly, saying in a mild tone, "Clean yourself off, and then come down to my office. We need to have a conversation." Then he turned and walked away from her, feeling as though his heart had been ripped from his chest. He headed down the winding stairs to his office. He poured himself a strong drink and sat down at his desk, putting his head in his hands for a long moment and letting a deep sigh flow from him. Then he took another long pull off of his whiskey and looked at the door, waiting for her.

Chapter 4

Kevin waited in his office and sipped his drink. He had just found his wife riding the gardener with heated abandon in her bed, and the only thing he could focus on was his drink. The gardener left and Kevin had solemnly instructed his wife to clean herself up and come down to his office for a conversation.

It was the first time he had been aware of her sleeping with someone else, but from the look of it, he suspected that it was not the first time it had happened. He promised himself that he would not let anger or jealousy rule the conversation. He would listen to her and give her as much benefit of the doubt as he could conjure up.

He waited patiently, and he began to wonder if she was taking her time to get to him because she felt ashamed and didn't want to face him, like a scolded child, or if she was disregarding him yet again, and dawdling because she felt like treating him with disdain.

He wondered for the better part of an hour before the office door opened and she strutted in, her skin-tight blouse and pants leaving nothing to the imagination. Her hair was long and loose and fell around her beautiful face in a dark cloud.

Kevin looked at his wife. "Would you like a drink?" he asked politely. She did not meet his gaze, but she nodded. He poured her a tumbler of whiskey and handed it to her, then sat opposite her on the sofa. As he looked at her, he thought that she did indeed look like a spoiled child.

"Ellen, explain to me why you have sunk to the depths of infidelity," he said quietly to her. He was so hurt and devastated inside that he had no idea where to begin with her, but he thought that an explanation was probably the best place to start.

She slumped her shoulders and silently looked away from him. She bit her lip and scowled and then she turned and glared directly at him. "If I have sunk as low as you say, then it's only because of you.

It's because you neglect me, you leave me alone all the time, you never pay attention to me and couldn't care less about me. I was driven to it. What else could I do? I'm a woman who has needs! You have no interest in seeing to those needs. You are too busy with your company, too busy in your office and rushing around in the middle of the night to tend to your wife, to give me any love and affection. You've left me no choice! None! You can't expect me to sit around up in my room alone like some prisoner in a white tower! It's completely your fault because you are a cold," she leaned closer to him, punching the words at him, "heartless bastard."

He listened to her without expression or reaction, absorbing what she had said. "How many times have you done it, Ellen?" He didn't want to know, but he found that he was compelled to ask.
"What makes you think that I've had to resort to that more than once?" she asked, suspicious of his motives.

"It's painfully obvious that this is not your first affair. You would be more emotionally wracked than you are right now if it was your first. It seems that you are more disappointed about being caught than having been reduced to finding love in your own bed rather than in your husband's." He maintained his calm, cool and collected tone, and it became clear that his doing so was irritating her and ruffling her feathers.

"Of course I'm disappointed that I was caught! What kind of a thing is that to say to me? Do you think it wouldn't bother me to be caught? Do you think I don't care if you see me in the arms of another man? I didn't want to do it to begin with, but you have left me no choice! Yes, I'm upset that you caught me, but not nearly as upset as I am that I had to resort to it in the first place!" She snapped at him, crossing her arms and legs tightly in front of her.

He took a deep breath. "I'm going to ask you again. How many other times has this happened?"

She tapped her foot and looked away from him. "Just a couple of other times," she replied sullenly.

"When did those times occur?" he asked, continuing his calm tone and manner, and seeing that it was unnerving her completely. He hadn't meant to unnerve her, but he didn't want to have an emotional confrontation with her, either.

Ellen lifted her chin and sniffed quietly. "Recently."

He leaned forward and rested his elbows on his knees. "Who was your lover the other times?"

She continued to look away, completely put out that she was being questioned in the manner that she was. "It was only ever the gardener. He was here, it just kind of happened." She shrugged her shoulders at him.

"Who instigated it?" Kevin asked, holding his eyes on her face as he read more of the truth there than she was willing to speak to him.

"Well, he did, of course. I would never start something like that. He was always coming on to me and he just wouldn't quit, and finally I couldn't fight him off anymore and I surrendered." Her expression looked as though he had wrestled her to the ground until she agreed to sleep with him as a last resort.

"You do realize he will no longer be employed here," Kevin stated, matter-of-factly.

She gaped and looked at him in frustration and irritation. "Well, where else is he supposed to work? You can't just kick him out like that! We need him around here!"

He was quiet a moment, taking a deep breath before responding, "He was temporary help, he can find work anywhere he likes, and we have other groundskeepers who will be able to fulfill the requirements of their positions without bedding the wife of their employer." His anger was beginning to surface.

She hissed a sigh and scowled again.

"Ellen, I need to know how you feel about our marriage. I need to know if you want to call it quits with us. If you aren't devoted to staying married and committed to creating a solid future with me, then we need to talk about dissolving our relationship." He leaned back and watched her.

Shock registered over her face and she finally turned to look at him fully. "Divorce? You can't be serious? Over a little thing like that? Whatever for?" Her body language changed completely and she turned herself to face him and leaned closer to him.

He looked down into the glass of whiskey in his hands, turning the glass slightly, and then lifting it to his lips to feel the burning liquid run over his tongue, warming him and soothing him before he looked at her and answered her.

"Ellen, every marriage goes through highs and lows, and this particular low that we are in has lasted for quite a long time. I do not believe that it is a low within a cycle any longer, but rather a habit with us.

"You don't seem to want to be intimate with me; you would rather find comfort in the arms of a stranger, a temporary employee, than in the bed of your husband.

"I have to know what you want out of our marriage, and I have to know if you intend to make the marriage work, or not. It takes two, and if we are going to make it through this, we both have to work at making it a strong partnership and we have to work at it together. That's what a marriage is; a partnership where both people make the marriage and the commitment to each other the biggest priority of their lives.

"I need to know if you can do that. I need to know how important this marriage and our future together is to you."

She pouted slightly and lowered her chin as she looked at him while he spoke to her.

"Ellen, I'm willing to put forth the effort with you. I made a commitment when we got married, when we said our vows to each other. I meant every word I said, and when I took you as my wife, I intended to be your husband and love you with all that is in me for the rest of my life.

"I meant it, you and me together forever. Now, we are going through a rough patch and I can only suppose that the hard times will continue as long as we are not both working together to make this marriage a success. I will give you more time together with me, if that's what you really want. I will give you any love and affection you need, if that's what you want.

"But if you want to go out on your own, if you want to sleep with other men, and if you want your freedom and independence, then I need to know now, because that kind of situation doesn't make a good marriage.

"If your freedom is what you want, then we don't need to be together, pretending to be married, and committed to each other. The best thing we can do for one another is to be honest and fair with each other and either cut off what is broken or work together to build it back up and make it strong and whole again. That choice is entirely up to you."

She leaned forward onto her knees and looked imploringly at him. "But Kevin, I don't want a divorce, I don't want to end what we have. I want to stay here with you as your wife. I just made a mistake! Do you understand that? I just slipped up, but I can commit myself to you. I can make you my priority and do this together.

"You can't sit there and tell me that the decision is all mine if you just finished telling me that our marriage is a partnership. If this is a partnership then the decision is half yours too, and you need to tell me what you want as well. You can't leave this whole thing up to me like that." She bit her lower lip and looked at him with wide dark eyes. "What do you want to do, Kevin?"

He took a deep breath and looked into his glass, and for a moment, he was honest with himself in his heart. He wanted Marina and

Maddie. He wanted to stand up and walk out of the house and go to his girls and be with them for the rest of his life.

His thoughts returned to the woman in front of him, who was wearing the ring that he placed on her hand when he told her that he wanted to spend the rest of his life with her. He made that choice; he was the one who decided that they should marry. He bought the ring, and he fell on his knees and asked her to spend her life with him. She could easily have married just about anyone else, but he asked her and she accepted him, and now she was asking him what he really wanted.

He knew he could not have what he really wanted. His morality and sense of devotion and commitment would not let him have it. He had to admit to himself that he had more than most people had; he had a wife, he had a child, and he hadn't been unfaithful in his commitment to his wife in order to create a legacy. He wasn't open and honest about it, but he had not lied and he did not cheat on her.

Kevin knew that to him, his word was the most important thing about him; his code, his honor, his commitment and the measure of his ethical fortitude. He had to keep his promise to Ellen. He pushed the thoughts of Marina and Maddie out of his mind and looked up at his wife.

"Of course I want to make it work with you; you are my wife, and I have promised myself to you for all of our lives. You are my priority. If you are willing to make this work, we will not talk about a divorce again, and we will work on rebuilding our marriage. What would you say to that?" he asked, with just a hint of weariness in his voice.

She stood up slowly, watching him like a cat, and walked over to him, then sat beside him on the couch. "Kevin," she said, leaning her arm on the back of the sofa and facing his side, "what if we did try to rebuild this. Sort of refresh our marriage and start over again. What if we went on a honeymoon together, and focused on loving each other, and making this a strong marriage. I really don't want to lose you."

She leaned close to him and lifted her arm from the back of the sofa to run her fingers through his dark brown hair. "Can we do that, baby? Can we take a long trip and go somewhere? We can fall in love all over again and make it work… we can rediscover all the things about each other that we really love. Let's do that, okay?" she said with pure sweetness.

Kevin felt like his soul was tearing in two. "It really isn't a very good time for me to leave right now, perhaps we could work on this close to the house… you know, sort of stay here at home and work on it together. What do you think about that?" he asked hopefully as a pit of fear, worry, concern and dread formed in his stomach and began to spin. His daughter was brand new. He wanted to be as near to her as he could be, as often as he could be.

She drew her eyebrows down in frustration and pouted again, pushing her red lips out in protest. "But Kevin! You just said you wanted to do everything you could to make this work! I ask you for this one thing, to put us first, to make us a priority and to come away with me so it will be just the two of us and we can leave business behind, we can leave the house behind, we can focus on just each other, and you tell me no!

"That's not building together; that's keeping things exactly as they are! Come on, honey, please do your part! Take me somewhere nice so we can really start to rebuild this marriage! I don't want to lose you!" She placed her hand on his thigh and began to move it up slowly toward his groin. He placed his hand over hers and stopped her.

"I just have a lot going on here right now and it would be very difficult to leave. Perhaps if we left in a month or so… you know, I could wrap up what I'm working on now and then leave with less on my mind. I could focus on you more. Could you give me more time before we agree to go anywhere?" he asked, the pit inside him swirling darkly and pulling at him with clawed fingers. Maddie's tiny face was lodged in his thoughts. He couldn't stand the idea of being away from her so soon, and for any length of time.

Ellen leaned very close to his ear and pressed her body up against his. "Kevin, you are the one who wants to fix our broken marriage. You are the one who just said that you would do anything to make it right, that you would spend more time with me, make me feel loved and give me affection.

"This is what I want. I want you with me, away from home on a second honeymoon. I want it now. Do this for me. Let's fix our marriage. Take me away on a long romantic trip and really try to do this. Okay? For me? Come on. Let's leave tomorrow, okay?" she pleaded with a sultry velvet voice.

He knew there was no way out of it. She would not let it go, and she was right; he had made all those promises and he had agreed to put her first and try to rebuild their marriage. He was shocked that she wanted to remain married to him, but he thought that perhaps she was right and she had just made a mistake with her infidelity. He shook his head and covered his face with his hands for a moment as she raked her fingers back and forth through his hair.

There was no way out of it for him. He sighed deeply and looked at her. "Can you give me a day, please? I would ask for one day so that I can get everything I can wrapped up here before we leave. Would that be alright?"

She squealed and grinned. "Then we can go?" she asked with childlike excitement.

He nodded. "Then we can go."

She hugged him tightly around his neck and pressed her chest into his face as she climbed onto his lap. "Yes! You can have one day. That will give me time to shop for the trip. Oh baby, let's go somewhere tropical, please?" She slid both of her legs over his and straddled his lap, leaning close to him, holding his face in her hands.

He looked up at her and felt as though he was completely submerged in utter defeat. There was just nothing for it; nothing at all that he could do about it. He would have time to say goodbye to Marina and Maddie, and then he would have to go.

"I think two weeks would suffice. We can go somewhere tropical for two weeks. You like Costa Rica. Would you like to go there? Or Hawaii maybe?" he asked with a touch of sadness in his voice.

She bounced a little on him. "Oh! Hawaii! We haven't been there in ages. I love Honolulu. Get me a really nice house there and we'll go have a nice time and fall back in love and make everything right again. Okay? Do that for me?" she purred, looking at him with happy eyes.

He wondered, as he gazed up into her delighted face, if perhaps he really had been at fault for the dissolution in their marriage; if she was right and their troubles were based on his absence and focus on his business, rather than on her. The thought of his failure toward her in their marriage made him feel horrible. How could he have let her down?

She slid closer to his crotch and leaned down to kiss him, but he pulled away and held her at a slight distance from him. "Ellen," he said quietly, "I do want to try to fix our marriage, but you did just leave another man in your bed and I'm not quite ready to be physically romantic with you quite so soon. We can try to rekindle that flame when we are on our trip, alright?"

She pouted and looked as though she might try to seduce him anyway, but she saw that he was serious and she pushed herself up off him and pulled him to his feet.

"Okay, baby, but you and I are going to make this work." She smiled at him and tipped her face up, pressing her lips against his gently and slowly, closing her eyes and reminding him of the sparks that had once flown between them.

Kevin made an effort to kiss her back and simultaneously try to keep the images of her wildly riding their gardener in her bed out of his mind while she was so close to him. He had agreed, he had committed, and he was going to put his wife and his marriage first. He just had no idea how he was going to do it.

Chapter 5

He went to his room alone and saw that Marina had called him twice and sent him text photos of Maddie and herself. They looked beautiful and stole his breath away He ached for them, wishing with everything in him that he could be with them, but that was not possible because he had committed to righting the wrongs of his marriage and making it work.

He texted Marina back and said he would see them both the following morning. He wanted to explain in person and try to face her when he told her that he was going to be leaving with his wife for two weeks. He undressed and fell into his bed alone; sad yet determined to make it all work.

The next morning he showered, dressed, and drove to Marina's early, hoping to have as much time with her and Maddie as he could. It did not feel like the traffic would ever move out of his way, or that the car would go fast enough, or that he could get to her house quickly enough to lay his eyes on them, but it did finally happen, and he stepped through her bedroom door and saw her laying in her new bed with Maddie sleeping next to her.

He went to her side of the bed and she leaned up and hugged him. He closed his eyes and breathed her in, soaking in her sweetness and beauty. Kevin kissed her cheek lightly and could not help himself from crawling into the bed with her, beside her, spooning her slightly and looking over her shoulder at their daughter in her blissful slumber.

"How is she doing?" he asked in complete happiness as he watched her.

Marina seemed happy and simultaneously worried. "She's wonderful; she's been eating really well and resting well. I am just so in love with her. It is the most amazing thing I've ever felt. We're so lucky to have her." She turned her head and smiled at him.

He frowned and looked at her carefully. "Is something wrong?" he asked with a concerned tone.

She sighed. "Yeah, there's something I wanted to tell you about, and that was why I called you last night, but I am glad I can talk with you about it in person. It's better that way."

He sat up in the bed and looked at her. "What is it? What's going on?"

She rolled over on her back against the pillows and looked up at him. He really was so beautiful, so elegant and refined. It was like looking at a man who had walked off the cover of a GQ magazine, and he always made her feel like she was the most important person in the world to him, next to their daughter.
Butterflies began to dance slowly in her stomach as she gazed up at him leaning over her. She reminded herself yet again not to fall in love with him. She had been fighting her growing feelings as much as she could, telling herself that he was married and he was going to stay that way, they had made and agreed to an arrangement and she couldn't change it now that things felt different for her.

She had to keep their relationship good and strong so that she and her daughter would have the best possible bonds with him. She would not risk the chance of having awkward issues with him. There was also the fact that she had some unexpected news to tell him, and she was not sure what his reaction would be. She took a deep breath and began.

"Kevin, I got a letter in the mail yesterday. It was from Lamar. He wants to talk with me. He sent me his phone number and he asked me to call him. He said he has some things he needs to work out with me." She held her breath after she said the words, waiting to see what would happen.

There was almost nothing else she might have said that would have affected Kevin as much as that statement did.

He held the upheaval of emotion in check within him. It was as though everything inside him had exploded in sheer panic. No! he thought; don't talk to him. No! he thought, don't respond, see him, listen to him, you are mine now. He left, he can't have you, he can't be around Maddie, he can't and you can't…

But then he remembered that she was not his, lying there beneath him with her long dark curls framing her beautiful dark face and her blue-gray eyes. The panic shot through him and it was all he could do not to lean down and kiss her.

He wanted to show her that he needed her, that what he felt for her had begun to grow far beyond the friendship that they had agreed to have. He longed to press his lips to hers, but he knew he had to let her live her own life, because he was married. He had no claim to her, no right to tell her, or even ask her, not to be with anyone else or to talk with any other men.

He was married, and he was about to tell her that he was leaving on a trip with his wife for two weeks.

His silence almost strangled him for a long silent moment as she watched him carefully, trying to gauge his reaction. He took a deep breath.

"Didn't you tell me that the two of you are finished for good?" he asked her as simply as he could, lest the emotions that were roiling through him erupt through his mostly calm surface.

 She watched his eyes and saw that he looked tormented inside. She felt so badly for him, but she knew she had to be honest.

"I did say that, but when I read the letter, I felt really sorry for him and I thought about it last night, slept on it, and this morning I called the number he gave me."

The pit in Kevin's stomach became molten lava. Don't kiss her, he thought repeatedly. Do not try to keep her; she is not yours to have.

Do not try to claim this woman's heart… he thought over and over again in his mind as he looked down at her.

"How did the phone call go?" he asked with as level a tone as he could muster.

She could see that he was having some internal difficulty, but she did not know why. She thought it might be because he was worried about Lamar being around Maddie.

"It was awkward, at first, but we talked for a long time and the more we talked, the easier it got. He was surprised about Maddie. He said he was happy for me. He said he wants to see me and meet her. I told him I wanted to talk with you about that first, because you are her daddy. He's going to check back with me to see if it's alright if he comes over." She felt compelled to tell him the truth.

Kevin swallowed as his heart began to pound in his chest. "Do you want him to come over?" he asked quietly.

She was silent a moment; pensive, thoughtful, and then she nodded. "I think I do. I want him to see that I'm doing well, that I have thrived and grown and that my life is incredibly blessed now."

He knew he could not deny her what she wanted, and he knew he had no right to ask her to do otherwise. "Well, the timing certainly worked out well for a visit from him."

She cocked her head to the side. "What do you mean?" she asked curiously, sensing there was something he hadn't yet told her.

He pursed his lips a moment and looked into her eyes. "It seems that my wife wants to go on a trip. I wish she would wait; I really find the thought of being away from Maddie unbearable for two weeks, especially now when we are just getting to know her and she is so small. I want to be here to help you with her, but this trip is something I just can't get out of, and I have to go.

"We're leaving tomorrow. We'll be gone for two weeks. When we're back, you two will be the first people I come and see. So, it works out that Lamar wants to visit with you, because you will need the help and I will be gone." He sighed with his closing comment. "I will miss you both," he added, touching her hand lightly.

She warmed to his touch and it softened the blow of his being gone for what seemed such a long time. He hadn't been gone from her for more than three or four days since she was seven months pregnant. She wrapped her hand around his and gave him a genuine smile.

"I'll miss you, too, but maybe this trip with your wife will be a good one for you both," she said selflessly. She did hope it was a good trip, but it pinched her heart painfully to know that he would be somewhere else with his wife rather than there with her and their daughter.

He stroked his thumb over her hand. "Please call me and keep in touch while I'm gone. I'll want updates all the time about how you are both doing, and if you need anything at all, let me know, or let Mac know, and you will be taken care of right away."

She sat up and wrapped her arms around his neck, holding him closely and speaking softly into his ear. "You always take such good care of me. Thank you." They both needed a long hug. Finally, knowing her hug rule about not being the first to let go, he moved his arms away, releasing her reluctantly.

"Be careful with Lamar. I wouldn't want you to be hurt again. I know it's not my place to say anything, but I want you to be alright." He smiled his best at her, and she nodded.

"I will be careful. I think it's really more of a closure for us both. We will keep it easy and friendly. No reason to do otherwise." She smiled at him and just then, their daughter woke up. Maddie fussed for a few minutes until she was changed. Marina fed her, and Kevin watched them, fascinated and completely spellbound by the beauty of nature, and of his child and her mother.

He burped his daughter and changed her again before he carefully placed her in her bassinet. Marina walked with him to the door and they hugged each other tightly for a long while. He turned his face to hers and kissed her cheek, lingering there just a moment, wishing that it could be much more than just her cheek that he kissed. She, wishing for the same, kissed his cheek in return and smiled up at him in a friendly way, and closed the door behind him as he left.

She leaned her forehead against it and took a deep breath, reminding herself that he would never be hers, that her heart needed to focus on herself and her baby girl, and that she absolutely had to stop the romantic thoughts of him as they moved through her mind.

He was completely off limits, and that was the most important thing to remember. Perhaps Lamar would give her something else to focus on when she called him to tell him he was welcome to visit them.

When Kevin and Ellen left for their trip the next day, he was quiet and slightly withdrawn, quite a contrast compared to her delighted and bubbly effervescence.

She had gone shopping and purchased an entire new wardrobe for their two-week vacation, including a new swimsuit and a few outfits for each day they were there. She also bought new luggage to take all of it with her. Her pack of tiny dogs got travel outfits, as well, and she purchased new carrying bags for them.

Kevin said nothing about her extravagance. He spent much of his time trying to keep his thoughts on the purpose of the trip, and that was to repair his marriage and strengthen his relationship with his wife. Each time a thought of Marina and Maddie came into his mind, he had to push it away, albeit reluctantly, so that he could use his energies to focus on his wife. He clung to his morality like a life raft in an ocean of confusion and emotion.

They flew to Oahu and a car took them to an enormous house on the beach where they would be staying. Ellen persuaded Kevin to abandon the ocean for the first day and take her shopping in Honolulu. He loved the island, but he wanted to see more of the natural wonder of it and she was more interested in the teeming city offerings.

He relented to her requests and followed her around as she went from boutique to boutique, shopping from one place to the next and said nothing about what he wanted to do and where he wanted to go, and she didn't ask.

They attended a luau on their first evening on the island, and afterward, when they got back to their house, he went for a walk on the beach to watch the moon rise over the dancing sea. She came out to him a short while after he went out, and found him sitting in the dry sand, watching the waves wash in and the moonlight glinting off of the water.

"What are you doing out here?" she asked. "It's dark!"

He looked over his shoulder at her and she stood beside him as he sat. "I'm just enjoying the scenery, watching the ocean in the night. Would you like to sit with me? It's quite relaxing."

She made a face. "No! I can't see what's in the sand; there's not enough light out. What are you looking at anyway? The water is dark. God knows what's swimming around out there in that black water; it's creepy. Come back inside with me. Come on." She insisted, giving the sea a look of suspicion.

He knew she wouldn't be talked into staying out on the beach with him, so he sighed and stood up beside her. "Alright. What would you like to do?" he asked, trying to hide his melancholy.

She smiled at him and took his hand, leading him back into the house. She walked with him to their bedroom and stopped him beside their bed. It was the first bed they had shared in a very long time. He stood silently before her and she smiled silkily at him and looked up at him through her eyelashes, then reached up and began to unbutton his shirt.

He didn't expect her to try to seduce him, to want him, to have a physical interest in him, but there she was, pushing his shirt off him and running her hands over his chest. Kevin focused intently on her, remembering how it had been when they had first fallen in love, and tried to discover things about her that he could love again. He lifted his hands and covered hers with them, holding them as she ran them over him.

Ellen smiled up at him and began to press her lips on the solid wall of his chest, kissing him softly and tasting him intermittently. He watched her, then lifted his hand to her head and ran his fingers through her long dark hair. Her beauty was entrancing, but somehow he found it tainted, and it took all his will to look at her with eyes that did not judge; eyes that could see her as a lover and wife all his own.

She slipped her hands up to his head and pulled him to her to kiss him; her lips were soft and inviting, and her kiss was warm. When he let it, it began to feel like possibility. It felt as though perhaps if he tried… if they both tried, maybe something could be built again between them. She had not been so intimate with him in long ages. He moved his hands to her cheeks and held her face gently to his as he opened his mouth and kissed her back, tasting her lightly, and moving his mouth tenderly over hers. It was like finding a new lover, one he had never known, but somehow perhaps, remembered from a dream had in time long past.

Sparks of heat began to alight within him and his breath grew deep as his heart began to pound in his chest. She moved her hands to his waist and his clothing fell away from him. His kisses grew deeper and warmer, and he closed her in his embrace, his body remembering how she felt, and how much he had wanted her for so long. Kevin traced his kisses along her jaw and her neck, toward her collarbone, and his fingertips moved lightly from her cheeks down her neck to the edges of the top she was wearing.

He lifted it carefully over her head and released it to the floor, and then gazed at her nude body before him. He pushed the thoughts of her with another man from his mind and steadied his attention to the present, to the stunning woman before him, to his wife. He touched her delicately, caressing her rounded breasts and tracing her curves with the tips of his fingers. She drew in her breath and smiled at him, watching him as though she might begin to purr.

Kevin lowered his mouth to hers again, kissing her softly as his hands moved over her body slowly, feeling every part of her and rediscovering the flesh he had not known in so long. It created a hunger in him that began to grow stronger and brighter and his desire for her began to mount.

She reached for him, closing her hands around his stiffening erection, massaging him and making him gasp with need for her. His kisses moved to her neck, pressing his lips to soft warm areas that made her hold him tighter, and he breathed in the scents in her hair, closing his eyes and creating new memories of love with her.

Ellen pulled him down onto the bed with her and as he lay down, she climbed on top of him, straddling him, and moving herself against the outside of him in a teasing arousal. Without thinking or realizing it would happen, Kevin flashed back to the scene of her romping on top of the gardener this same way, and he grasped her hips in his hands and held her fast.

"Ellen," he breathed in a pained whisper, "Stop… please, let's do this another way."

She started and looked down at him in surprise, but she let him turn and roll them over until she was underneath him. He spread her knees apart and in moments was pushing himself inside of her. His eyes closed, his body was enveloped in her heat and in her embrace.

He kissed her, looking to lose himself in her fully, and she wrapped her legs around him and moved with him as he entered her over and over.

Their heated skin grew dewy in the warm tropical night air and as the flames of desire and passion grew hot and boundless, he closed his eyes and in his mind, all he could see was Marina. He saw her dark breasts, her beautiful blue-gray eyes, her sweet warm smile, and he felt her arms around him.

He was so overcome with desire and emotion, with love and need, that he let the fantasy become as real to him as it could be. He moved with urgency and hunger inside of his wife, but imagining Marina beneath him, in his arms, kissing him back, and his mouth closed over Ellen's flesh ravenously as he saw the mother of his child in his mind.

He knew he should not think of her, he knew full well that he had no business imagining her beneath him, his body inside hers, her flesh in his mouth. But once she came into his thoughts, once it felt as though she may be there with him, he could not deny himself the moments he so desperately wanted with her.

He wanted their encounter to last, he wanted to keep his eyes closed and pretend that she was there making love with him, that the soft moans he heard were hers, and that the woman clinging to him as he moved passionately within her was Marina.

But his body would not let it last, his ache for her was too great, his love and desire too strong, and his body could not contain the love he longed for so desperately. He shuddered as his body reached orgasm and his lips, pressed passionately against the skin of her neck, spoke softly with his heart's desire, "Marina..." he whispered.

Ellen opened her eyes and pushed at his chest, looking at him with surprise and amazement. "What did you say?" she asked with shock.

It was too late that he comprehended his mistake as he looked down into the bewildered and stunned face of his wife, the woman he had meant to make love to, the woman he was trying to rebuild a bond with, and the pounding in his head felt like a freight train racing forward, rails rattling and whistle screaming.

"I said I want to make love with you at the marina, where the boats are docked," he volleyed for a lame save. She lowered her eyebrows at him and pursed her lips. He continued to row upriver. "Let's go rent a sailboat overnight and make love out by the marina, rocking in the waves and be lulled to sleep in each other's arms. I want more romance with you than this. We can do better. We have a marriage to save."

She bought it, he thought. The tension in her face eased and his heart began to slow down as he watched her smile at him and lean up to kiss him. "Oh," she said, her Cheshire cat smile turning up the corners of her mouth. "I thought you were calling out another woman's name. I was worried for a minute." She kissed him with a sultry slowness and kept her eyes open as she did.

"I really don't like boats that much. You know that. Why would I think that was romantic? The ocean is creepy at night. All that black water, and who knows what, swimming, just waiting to get you. That is not romantic at all. I would rather have you here in this soft plush bed, surrounded by pillows and maybe some candles and music. That would be romantic." She kept the masked joker smile on her face and moved out from beneath him.

"Also, while we're talking about what we like, I happen to like being on top. It makes me feel like I am more in control, and it turns me on. Why didn't you let me stay on top? What's the big deal with you needing me underneath you?"

He wasn't sure if he could say it to her. He wanted to; he wanted to say that he could not get the image eradicated from his mind... the image of her straddled over the gardener's hips, gyrating away at him in her bed, and he didn't want to be the man under her in place of the gardener. He could not say it. "I just like to be on top, too," he said softly and smiled at her. Kevin kissed his wife's cheek and rose from their bed, walking to the shower.

The hot water poured over him and steam billowed around his muscular body. He closed his eyes. It was difficult making love with so many people in their bed. The mental image of the man he'd seen his wife with pushing his way into the sheets with them, Marina appearing beneath him in his mind, and, of course, the two of them who were physically there.

He felt horribly ashamed that he had let himself fantasize about Marina. That was no way to repair his marriage, and it was certainly no way to keep his relationship with Marina a platonic one.

He closed his eyes and his image of her beneath him returned full force. He could see her body in his mind, her beautiful eyes and warm, loving smile. He longed to feel her dark skin against his, her arms holding him, her hands clinging to his body as he entered her over and over, as he kissed her, tasted her, and loved every inch of her…

His body responded to his deep desires and he realized that he had stiffened into an erection once again. He groaned and turned the temperature of the water down, letting the coolness of it wash away his aching need for a woman he would never have.

He thought about his mistake in calling out her name at the height of his orgasm, and was grateful that Ellen was not bright enough to realize that he had lied to her. He felt shame for the lie as well as for his pretense in making love to his wife when he was actually thinking of another woman. He never lied to Ellen or anyone else. He was staunch about telling the truth, and luckily, Ellen knew that about him, or he might have had more concerns on his mind.

Kevin stepped out of the shower and dried off, then headed to bed to find his wife already asleep. He looked at her, lying there with her leg over the sheet, her dark head sunken into the pillow, her full sweet lips slightly parted as dreams surely flitted through her mind.

She really was a beautiful woman and she deserved the love and devotion of her husband. He vowed to himself as he stood over her, watching her slumber, that he would be as good as he could to her, that he would live up to the promises that he made to her during their wedding, and that she would know his love was for her in the future.

He crawled in next to her and watched her sleep for a while, wondering what she was dreaming about, wishing that he had not betrayed her in his mind when they were making love, and he fell asleep looking at her beautiful face.

When he awoke, she was still sleeping. He reached over to touch her cheek, and she slowly opened her eyes and looked at him. A smile began to spread over her lips and, watching her intently, his eyes locked on hers, he leaned over to her and kissed her, softly at first, and then more urgently as morning's desire overtook him.

He rolled onto his back, pulling her with him so that she was astride him where she wanted to be, and he entered her, watching her and thinking only of the woman he was with as his hands and lips gently caressed her body. He made passionate love to her, and she reveled in the attention he lavished on her.

The remainder of their second honeymoon was spent in harmonious happiness; holding hands, enjoying their time together and sleeping beside one another. Kevin believed by the end of it that perhaps they had managed to save their bond once again, and that the two of them, committed to one another, might spend the rest of their lives in love and married, making a future together until the end of their days.

Ellen basked in his singular attention and devotion, reveling in being the center of his world.

When Kevin left, Marina had felt as though she might have lost what she had never had, and she kept reminding herself that she had decided not to fall in love with a married man. She blamed it on the hormones that were raging rampantly throughout her body, and she focused all her time and energies on her sweet baby daughter.

She sent Kevin texts and photos, and for the first few days, she heard back from him constantly. But as the days went on, his responses to her were shorter and less frequent, and she told herself that she must hold tight to their friendship without looking for more, so that they could offer their daughter the best possible upbringing.

Four days after Kevin left, Lamar came to her house and knocked on the door. She felt her heart leap into her throat when she opened the door and saw him standing there. Time had changed him. He had gone from being a thick boy to being a tall, slender, toned and trim man.

His body and face had matured, and his demeanor was completely different. He was quieter, more at ease, more at peace, and perhaps a bit more accepting of his own faults. The fires of youth seemed to have given way to the patience of time and age.

She invited him in and for an awkward moment, neither of them knew what to do, but then he reached for her and hugged her, loosely at first, and then as the familiarity of his hands on her body came over them both, he pulled her close to him and held her tightly.

"I'm so sorry, Marina. I could never say that enough to you. I wish so much that I had gone that day, that I hadn't talked myself out of loving you and keeping you as my wife for the rest of my life. I'm so sorry." He released her and looked down into her eyes as tears fell down both of their cheeks. "Can you forgive me?" he asked in a choked whisper.

She was overwhelmed with emotion, and because she had let go of the anger years before, she knew she could, and so she said so to him. "Yes, Lamar, I will. I forgive you. I know you didn't hurt me on purpose."

He pulled her closely to him and held her to his heart for a long time, until both of them had cried through the emotion and were able to breathe deeply again, then he let her go and she stepped away from him.

He smiled down at her and wiped the tears from his eyes. "So it looks like things are going really well for you." His gaze encompassed the room and her, and he smiled. "I'm glad to see it. You must be doing alright. I want that for you. I want you to be happy."

84

"I am happy." She meant it, mostly. She was happy. Other than being in love with a married man whom she could not have, she was happy. She had a beautiful baby girl, a lovely home, she was finishing a great education, and she was going to be well taken care of for the rest of her life. Things were very good.

"The baby is just the sweetest little thing in the world. She is everything to me." Marina could not help grinning. Maddie always made her grin.

Lamar smiled and looked a bit nervous. "Would it be alright if I saw her?" he asked carefully.

Marina looked at him for a moment, watching him, reading his expression and his eyes, and then she smiled and indicated the sofa in the living room, "Yes, you can. Go ahead and have a seat there, and I'll get her. She's in the other room."

He sat, gazing around the room anxiously, and Marina went into her bedroom.

She emerged a few moments later, her arms filled with colorful blankets, and she sat near Lamar on the sofa, tilting her arms so that he could see the sleeping angel in them.

He grinned immediately and looked up at Marina. "She's beautiful, just like her mama," he said with complete pleasure.

Marina nodded proudly. "She has my eyes. She is so perfect; I just love everything about her." She raised Maddie to her face and kissed her softly.

Lamar watched her intently for a long moment and then looked away, choked up a bit.

"What is it?" she asked him, concern on her lovely face.

He turned to face her again and wiped his hand over his eyes to catch the tears there.

"She's beautiful, Marina, and if I had done what I said I would do, she'd be mine, and we would be a family. It's a lot for me to think on, that's all." He sat up straight and took a deep breath, letting it out slowly. "I hope you don't mind me asking, who's gonna raise her up?"

"Her father and I are," Marina said quietly.

He frowned slightly and nodded. "Are you two together? You're going to marry him?" he asked, obviously not really wanting to know the answer to his questions.

She shook her head. "No, we're just really close friends. He's with someone else, but he's around for her and he's there for me, too."

Lamar shook his head in confusion. "That doesn't make any sense to me."

Marina thought to herself that not all the real details made much sense to her either, but she kept it to herself.

He placed his hands on his knees, took another deep breath, and looked at her. "If you aren't seeing her father, are you seeing anyone else?"

She felt her body freeze from her hair down; everything in her went still and she could hear her heart pound almost in time with the clock ticking on the mantle over her fireplace.

"I'm not seeing anyone. I am happy with my life as it is, just Maddie and I and her daddy coming around to see her. That is enough. That's fine with me," she said, trying not to sound cold.

He nodded. "Well, maybe it would be alright then if we went out to dinner sometime, you know, just to talk. I spent a lot of time without you, it felt like it left a hole in my life, in my heart… and I want to fill it back up. I want the hole filled. I want you back in my life. Even if we are just friends.

"You are such a strong, beautiful woman, Marina, you are like sunshine walking around on the earth, and it is mighty cold without you. I just wondered if we can change that." He spoke honestly and kept his eyes on hers the whole time he talked, which made her wish she could believe what he said, even though her trust for him was gone.

She didn't know quite what to say to him. She rocked Maddie a little more fervently, in essence rocking herself a bit more, just for the comfort. She turned her head and looked down at her baby, unsure what to make of his request. She had trusted him before, and he had let her down; he had left her waiting at the altar for a husband that never came.

Now here he was again, asking for her trust, her time, and her company. And for what? What benefit would he be in her life, she wondered. She realized that if she could not answer that question, then she did not know, and if she did not know, then she could make no firm decision on it.

"We'll see," she finally said in a hushed tone. "What do you want, Lamar?" she asked with uncertainty.

He never took his eyes from her. "I just want you back in my life. However that might be."

She sighed deeply and nodded. "Alright, Lamar, alright. We can see how it goes. Maybe we can be friends. We can try." She acquiesced and a smile spread over his face.

"Good. That's good. I'll show you how different I am now. I've changed a lot, Marina, you'll see that in no time at all." He nodded his head.

"I can already see it," she replied, looking at him with a smile. "You've grown up. That is clear. We'll figure out the rest as we go along, I guess."

He looked at Maddie again. "Can I hold her?" he asked, his eyes meeting hers.

She paused a moment and then, pushing away the thought that this might have been his baby she was handing to him, she placed Maddie in his arms. He held her close to his chest for a long while, looking down at her, rocking her gently, and then he gave her back to her mother.

"She's really something else," he said with a sad smile.

"She really is," Marina agreed.

Lamar rose to leave and Marina put Maddie down and walked him to the door. He wrapped his arms around her and held her tight, and per her usual rule, she didn't let go until he did.

"I've missed those hugs," he said quietly in her ear before letting her go fully, and then he kissed her cheek softly. "You are more beautiful than you've ever been."

She looked down for a moment and then her eyes rose to meet his. "Thank you." That was all she said.

He left and she closed the door behind him and watched him walk away from the window while she held Maddie in her arms. The significance of his back walking away from her and leaving her alone, was not lost on her. She hoped that someday, that would not be the dominant thought in her head when she looked at him.

He was back the next day, and the day after that, and the day after that. Each day he came to see her and each day he brought flowers, lunch or some thoughtful gift for her or for Maddie. Each day she grew more comfortable with him, but she began to grow leery of his constant presence. The communication from Kevin had slowed just a bit, and Lamar was becoming a constant presence in her home.

He kept a respectful distance from her, but each day that distance grew shorter and shorter. She was just a little more concerned with what he wanted from her. Finally, she knew she would need to talk with him about it.

They were standing in the kitchen and Maddie was sleeping in the living room. Marina poured him a cup of coffee and when she turned to look at him, she saw that his eyes had not left her at all since they had entered the room.

"Lamar, we need to talk," she said with a smile, hoping she sounded kind.

He took a step toward her. "That we do, Marina."

She felt butterflies suddenly erupt within her and begin to zoom about as though it was a blizzard of them swirling everywhere. Her heart began to race and he took another step toward her, making her catch her breath as she looked up at him in uncertainty.

"You've been coming over often… um, every day actually…" she managed as he stepped toward her again and stopped right in front of her.

"…um, and I…" she forced herself to take a breath and look up into his dark brown eyes which were locked on her face, "I just wanted to remind you that we are just friends, Lamar." She lost her voice at that point, because he had reached his hand up and taken her chin in his fingers. Her heart pounded against her chest and blood rushed through her.

Her breath became short and she felt almost helpless as he gazed down at her, inches from her face.

"We are friends. Good, old friends. Now you are a momma, and I love that about you, Marina. It has brought out a beauty in you that I never knew was there. I know Maddie's father is around sometimes, but there's no one here for you." He traced his thumb over her lower lip and she could not breathe.

"There's no one here to love you, and you are a woman who shines best when she is really loved." He lifted his hands to hold her face and lowered his lips to meet hers.

Everything in her went into alarm, and everything was on high alert as he pressed his lips to hers softly, kissing her with a gentle tenderness. She felt like every natural disaster in the world was going off inside of her as his lips parted hers and when his tongue met hers, she closed her eyes and a soft cry emerged from somewhere near her heart, escaping from her body, only to be muffled by Lamar's kisses.

She didn't know what she ought to do and confusion twisted through her as tiny embers of remembrance began to glow in the depths of her. He tasted her deeply and she gasped, submitting and kissing him in return, uncertain if it was what she really wanted, but feeling the electric wires in her body go live with his touch.

Lamar moved his hands from her face to her shoulders, pulling her close to him, and then slid them slowly down the sides of her full breasts and around her waist, drawing her forward until they were pressed firmly against one another. She wanted to pull away; she wanted to run, having felt ultimate rejection from this man. Yet, the magnetic pull of his familiar and unfamiliar mouth on hers was dynamic. She had loved him more than she had ever loved anyone, and she had been hurt more by him than anyone else had ever hurt her. It was a powerful paradox, and one that created a vortex of confusion in her.

As if stepping in like a guardian angel, Maddie woke and cried for her mother, and Marina instantly pulled away from Lamar, both of them gasping for air. Marina felt her world slowly right itself again. She walked into the living room and lifted her child into her arms, thanking her silently for her impeccable timing. She changed her and told Lamar that she needed to feed her, asking him if maybe he could visit another time, subtly implying that he needed to leave.

He nodded and leaned over to kiss her cheek before he walked out the door. Marina took Maddie to her bedroom and climbed into the bed to feed her. As she lay against the pillows, emotions overflowed out of her eyes and down her cheeks. He should have been her husband. He should have been Maddie's father, but he was not, and now she had no idea what to do with his affections and underlying intentions.

She and Maddie fell asleep again in the bed where Kevin had slept beside them. Marina laid there, missing him terribly and wishing he were with them now. She knew it would only complicate matters more, but at least she knew where she stood with him. She wanted him, he was married, and she could not have him. Those were solid lines. Those were boundaries. There were rules in place.

There were no rules with Lamar; he was a wild card, a dangerous possibility, and she had no idea how to handle him or what to do.

Lamar returned the next day, as was his new habit, bringing two dozen red roses for Marina.

"I'm sorry if I went a little too far yesterday, Marina," he told her right away. "I don't want to hurt you. I want nothing for you and little Maddie but the best, but I just have all these feelings for you, and they are coming back so strong, stronger than they ever were before. I worry about you, lady, and I wonder what your life is going to be like raising this little girl on your own. I don't want you to be lonely." He kept a slight distance, but only slight.

"I'm so caught up in you, so bound up these feelings for you, Marina, you just pull at me like there's a gravity between us that I can't deny, and I want to be here with you both, however you will let me be here," he told her, watching her closely.

She kept herself a little way from him, keeping her eyes from connecting with him just a little more than she had been during his visits.

He helped her with Maddie as much as she would let him, and he helped her around the house. She knew he was showing her that he belonged there with her, but she just didn't know if she could make herself believe that it was real. She was not sure if she could trust him again and believe what he said.

Lamar was near to her every chance he got, touching her hand, her arm, her back, lingering and watching.

When she walked him to the door to tell him goodbye that day, he pulled her into another kiss, holding her closer than he had the day before and this time, when he let her go, he held her face in his hands and looked deeply into her eyes.

"Marina, I'm going to be honest with you. I think you probably know it, but I want you with me. I want to be your man, I want to help you raise Maddie and take care of you. I want that more than anything else in my life, and I am willing to do whatever it takes to make it happen.

"I'm not asking you to give me any kind of answer, but I want you to think about it. I want you to know just what it is that I am trying to do here. I want to build a family with you."

He kissed her as she stared at him in shock, her heart pounding and breaking almost simultaneously. "I have never stopped loving you, Marina, and you deserve to be loved, more than anything, all your life. You're my girl and I want you," he said earnestly, and then turned to leave as she stared after him with an open mouth and a torn heart.

Chapter6

Kevin's first priority when he and Ellen returned from their honeymoon was to see Marina and Maddie. He had missed them terribly over the course of the two weeks he had been gone. He realized that his constant focus on his phone texting to Marina had drawn the ire of his wife because of his lack of attention to her.

But it had also placed Marina squarely in his thoughts and dreams, and in order to focus on his goal of repairing his broken marriage, he had to keep her from constantly occupying his mind while he spent time with his wife.

The day they got back, Ellen went directly to her room and closed the door, and he felt as though somehow they might have returned to their old habits, but he was willing to give her the benefit of the doubt.

He, in turn, immediately went to Marina's. He saw a tall, solidly built, black man leaving her house when he arrived, and wondered about him as he entered. Lamar saw Kevin walking in and wondered the same thing.

Marina turned and saw Kevin in her doorway. Everything that had happened in the two weeks that they had been apart seemed to evaporate immediately, like morning fog; there for a moment, and gone the very next.

She rushed to him and hugged him tightly, and he locked his arms around her.

"I've missed you!" she said, in tears, unable to hold in her emotion.

He reached his hand up and stroked her long black curls. "I've missed you too, Marina. So much." His voice left him and he closed his eyes and breathed her in, pressing his face to her cheek and inhaling her scent. He kissed her cheek subtly, softly, and let his arms fall away from her. She smiled widely up at him and he saw the tears on her cheek.

His fingertips erased them and he tilted his head slightly. "What are the tears for? Are you alright?" Concern was beginning to bubble up in him.

"I'm fine. We're both just fine," she said grinning at him. "I just missed you so much, and it's been… busy around here." She shrugged and looked away from him. "Come see Maddie. She's getting so big already!"

He followed her and a seed of confusion and doubt began to grow in the pit of his stomach. They went into the bedroom and Kevin lifted Maddie from her bassinet, holding her close to his heart and rocking her as she slept. "I've missed you so much, sweet baby," he whispered, his hand covering her back. "God, I've missed you." He closed his eyes and for a moment, nothing in the world existed but the three of them together, and he was completely happy.

Then he kissed his daughter on her head and laid her back in her bassinet.

He sat on Marina's bed and looked at her. "What do you mean it's been busy? What's been going on here?" The seeds of concern were growing as he spoke.

She sat beside him and clasped her hands in her lap. "Well, Lamar came to visit and meet the baby," she started, uneasily.

Kevin nodded. "Yes?"

"And he's been coming back every day since," she continued, not looking at him until the words were out of her mouth.

Kevin felt everything in him tighten into a knot.

"Every day? Why would he do that?" he asked.

She drew a deep breath and looked at Kevin directly. "Well, he was on friendly terms when he first came in, but then he wanted to be around Maddie and me more, and so he came every day to see us, to spend time with us. Kevin, he has made it clear that he wants us."

Kevin could barely contain the chaos that overtook him inside, but he kept it in complete check and remained unruffled on the exterior. "What exactly does he want?" he asked, fearing that he already knew the answer.

She pressed her lips together and then shrugged. "He wants to be here with us. He wants to be a family."

He felt as though everything that was most precious to him in the world was being yanked away and it was the worst pain he had ever known. It ripped a hole through him and left a huge gaping darkness through which nothing but an arctic blast of cold could be keenly felt.

"What have you told him? What do you want?" he asked, not sure he wanted to know the answer.

She stood up, walked a few paces, and ran her hand over her forehead, then turned to face him. "I haven't answered him. He just said what he wants and he hasn't asked me what I want. I don't know what I want." But as she said it, she knew otherwise.

"Well, that's not entirely true; I do know what I want, but I can't have it, so the alternatives are to either be alone or to let him come back to me and be here with us."

Kevin stood up and looked sharply at her, doing his level best to keep his tone and his expression calm.

"Marina, anything you want, anything at all, is yours. I would give you anything or do whatever you want. Name it, and it is yours. What is it that you want?" he asked, stepping toward her, hoping that whatever it was could be the talisman that kept Lamar at bay and away from the woman he loved and his child.

She shook her head. "I can't tell you that, Kevin."

He began to feel desperation course through him and it was so thick that it felt like it was permeating his body. "You can have anything you want," he repeated, walking toward her until he reached her, standing just in front of her.

Marina's heart was breaking in her chest. She knew she couldn't have what she wanted, and she knew she could not admit it to Kevin. She felt like everything in her was splintering in pain.

"Kevin, I can't, so stop asking me, please." She could not stop a tear from rolling down her cheek and she tried to turn her head away from him so that he could not see it, but it was too late, and he lifted his hand to her cheek to wipe the tear away.

"Marina," he whispered and pulled her close to him, "Tell me, please. Tell me what it is you want. I will give it to you." He lifted her chin and looked into her eyes, trying to anchor himself to the floor so he wasn't completely lost in them.

She felt the frustration of her entanglement build until she could not hold it in any longer, and everything she had been keeping to herself erupted all at once in the firm hold of his arms.

"Kevin, I want you! Alright? I want to be with you. I love you. I want you here with me, helping me raise Maddie, holding me at night, loving me for the rest of my life. I want you! Are you happy now? I have admitted it.

"I cannot have you, you're married. I tried not to fall in love with you, and I've done my best. I just can't keep my heart from needing you, and it is tearing me up! Lamar came and he wants to be here with us.

"I want you and he wants to be in your place here, beside me with Maddie. Since you cannot be here and you don't want me like that, I have to decide whether I want to be alone and wish you were with me. Or I can let him in and at least have a little love in my life, even if it's not what I want."

She gushed everything out at him, and he stood there before her, awash in shock as her words registered meaning in his mind and in his heart.

He shook his head slightly in disbelief and suddenly grasped her face in his hands and drew her to him in a kiss, moving his mouth over hers in surprise, in need, in desire and disbelief, in utter happiness, in relief, and more than all of them together, in complete love.

Marina was stunned and still for a moment, but the warm touch of his lips on hers was like air to one who had been suffocating, and she drank him in, coming to life in his arms and feeling an exploding flame of desire and need ignite within her. She bound her arms around him and kissed him back as passionately as he was kissing her.

His hands moved from her face to her back, holding her to him tightly as his tongue found hers and they tasted the heat they had both longed for. It burned hotly and their bodies hardened against one another in need.

Kevin finally pulled his face away from hers and placed his hands on either side of her face. "Marina," he spoke in a ragged whisper, "I cannot tell you how much I have wanted to kiss you, to touch you, to love you. I love you, my sweet, wonderful, beautiful woman. I love you with all of my heart, and I have wanted you so desperately, but there is so much complication… so much…" he broke off and choked back his emotion.

"I know," she whispered, placing her hands over his to feel him.

"I'm married, and that is something I take very seriously. Ellen and I have recommitted ourselves to each other. I should not have even kissed you just now, and if that hurts you at all, I will never forgive myself for it, because I could never hurt you, but you have asked me for the one thing I cannot give you, and that is myself.

"Were it not for Ellen, I would be with you all of your days; I would spend my life with you, happily, blissfully, and love you every moment for the rest of eternity, but I am not free and I cannot give you that." He lowered his hands from her face and holding one of her hands, sat on the bed with her as tears rolled down both of their cheeks.

"I don't want Lamar here; I don't want him to be the dad that is around all the time, raising our daughter and loving you every night. I do not want him to have what I love more than anything in the world.

"He does not deserve it; he walked out on you and hurt you, and I couldn't bear for you to be hurt by anyone, including me. I can't ask you not to be with him; you are single, and I am committed and it's your right to be with someone so that you aren't alone. It would be wrong to ask you to sacrifice your happiness for my own selfish wishes, and I would never do that.

"The main thing is, I can't go back on my word and break my marriage vows. I gave my word, and I am nothing without my word. I might want you more than anything in this world, but I cannot break the biggest promise I have ever made in my life. Does any of that make sense to you at all?" he asked, hurt and relieved and happy and miserable all at once.

She could not stop the flow of tears running down her beautiful face, and he lifted his finger to wipe them away. "It doesn't make any sense, but I understand it. I want you, too… more than anything else, but I know I can't have you. It just makes this all the more difficult. Kevin, you say that you want to be with us more than anything, but you can't go back on your word… so where does that leave us?" She had never felt so confused.

He looked at her, this beautiful woman who had given him a daughter, who had taken more than all of his heart, who was generous and kind, who was beautiful and devoted, and who he could not imagine living his life without and he realized that word or no word, he had to make a difficult decision.

98

He could not leave her hanging in the balance, in limbo, making both of them miserable. He either needed to let her move forward with Lamar and remain married to Ellen, or go back on his word and divorce Ellen so he could be with Marina.

She watched him as her heart raced within her, and she knew he was working through thoughts that would probably determine the course of the rest of her life, and all she could do was hold his hand and wait for him.

She hoped beyond hope that he would choose her, that he would divorce his wife, although she had no right at all to hope for that, but the alternative of loving him from a distance while actually being so near him all of her life while they raised Maddie was almost more than she could bear.

Even if she did let Lamar into her life again as he wanted to be, it would be heart wrenching to be with one man and love another, especially one who was constantly in her life. She couldn't imagine it. It would feel like a betrayal of the heart.

He touched her cheek. "Marina, this is a huge decision. This affects so many lives. I want to ask you to let me think on it for a short time. Let me consider it so that I can make the best decision for all of us. Can you give me just a small amount of time? Please?" he asked almost desperately.

She felt like she was being held in a vacuum. "Yes," she said softly, turning her face to kiss his palm. He closed his eyes and lost himself in the intimacy of her lips upon his hand, wishing he could lay her back in her bed and make love to her, but knowing that for many reasons, it was not possible for them that day.

He pulled her to him and held her closely. "Thank you, Marina. Thank you. I will be quick with my decision, I promise you that. You won't have to wait long."

Then he cupped her face in his hands again and lost himself in her beautiful blue-gray eyes. "I love you so very much, lady. Much more than you will ever know. Thank you for your bravery and strength, and more than that, for your love." He leaned close to her, kissed her forehead, and then held her in his arms for a long while.

When Maddie awoke, he cared for her, changing her and holding her until it was time for her to nurse, and then he watched Marina as she fed their daughter and he knew that the choice he made would be the most significant choice of his life.

He kissed Marina's cheek when he left and then he drove home, the weight of the world on his mind and heart. He walked into the house and heard no noise, and he looked, but didn't see anyone.

A search upstairs revealed nothing; it was empty, so he went back down the stairs and wandered the whole of the first floor, ending his search in his office when he opened his door and saw Ellen sitting at his desk. She looked up at him from the large file of papers strewn over his blotter and shook her head.

"Well, well. Daddy's home," she said slowly and evenly, narrowing her eyes at him.

Kevin rushed to the desk and saw that it was Marina's file, filled with every bit of information about her and Maddie, including photographs and doctor's records from the very first day of the endeavor. He stopped in his tracks and looked at her.

She pushed his chair back from his desk and took a long pull from the full whiskey tumbler in her hand.

"So, this is Marina. This is who you were pretending to have in your bed while we were on our honeymoon." She pulled her feet up and placed two high-heeled shoes on the corner of his desk. "Here I was, so worried about being caught with the gardener, while *you*… you were out making a baby with another woman." She took another long drink and then took her feet off his desk and leaned over, looking at him sharply. "Sit down, daddy."

100

Kevin, his heart racing in his chest and his hands sweating, listened to her and sat down.

"You acted so holier than thou… so righteous… so never do wrong, and here you are breaking your word, breaking your vow, going outside of your marriage to procreate, and never breathing a word about it to me." She leaned far over his desk and glared at him.

"Liar!" she stabbed him with the word he knew to be true.

She stood up and the white satin robe she was barely wearing swished around her body as she turned sharply at the corner of the desk and came to the front of it, sitting on the front edge and placing her long nude legs up on the arm of Kevin's chair.

"And I thought you really meant it about fixing our broken marriage." She laughed and took another drink, and then leaned down toward him and whispered loudly, "That's okay, baby, because I didn't really mean it either. You see, when you caught me in my little love bed, I was worried that you were going to divorce me and leave me without my beautiful home here, and without all your money, and I just couldn't have that.

"Oh no! I have grown quite accustomed to being a billionaire's wife, and I do not intend to lose that. So, I went along with your little game of 'fixit', and I played the loving, devoted, redeemed wife, so that I could avoid a divorce, and all along…" she laughed and drank again, "All along, you were screwing this other woman and having a kid with her."

He looked up at her sharply. "I never slept with her, Ellen; it was an in vitro fertilization!"

She laughed at him. "Yeah, and here's why that's funny. No judge is going to believe that while I was here at the house being your devoted wife, you weren't out screwing this woman that you now have a child with, even if it was medically initiated, because you have been buying her things left and right, taking care of her, and spending all your time over there.

"You know what I found? Cell phone logs, darling, ohhh, you like to keep in contact with her all the time, don't you, baby? Yeah. I have so much information on you. You know what's going to happen? I'll tell you what's going to happen." She took another long drink and then leaned over to face him with an evil grin on her face.

"You are going to stop seeing her. Oh yes… you do not get to see her or your kid at all. If you so much as look in her direction or make a single call to her, I will drag your ass to court and take you for all the money you have, the house, the cars, your business… everything you have. Then what are you going to use to raise that kid? How will you ever pay for your woman then?"

She giggled and took a long drink. "Then, since I no longer have to pretend like I like you at all, I'm going to have all my lovers over here anytime I want, anywhere I want, and you don't get to say one single word about it."

He gaped at her in shock. She nodded and gave him a sly look. "Oh yeah, baby, there are several lovers. There have been all along. Since before I met you. I am really good at hiding them. Except for the gardener, of course. Oh well." She giggled again and took another drink.

Kevin thought that he would vomit. She leaned down and hovered her breasts near his face. "And baby, you don't get to talk to anyone about this. Not that gay assistant of yours, not your buddy Jacob, nobody. If anyone finds out, I drag your ass to court. If you go see your little girlfriend, I drag your ass to court. If you go see that bastard kid of yours, I drag your ass to court. You do anything without my permission, and you will lose everything. Got it?" She smiled at him, batting her eyelashes.

He sat there motionless and stunned. He had not realized so much about her, but he could not begin to see how he had misjudged her so completely. He had no idea who the woman standing before him was.

"Get out of my office," he said, standing up and suddenly becoming a wall before her.

She laughed at him and grinned, running her hand down the front of his suit and pulling his tied out from its tucked position. "Don't worry about hiding that file, baby. I have copies of all of it, safely tucked away. You don't stand a chance against me, so don't even think of doing anything stupid or you're going to lose everything you've got."

Ellen giggled again and walked out of the office, stopping to look over her shoulder long enough to say, "Thanks for the honeymoon, baby." Then she closed the door behind her.

Kevin went behind his desk and looked at the file. Everything was in it. His phone records were out, every purchase he had made for Marina was out, and all of it looked as though he had been having an affair with her the whole time, or at least since she was seven months along.

He was more than devastated. He began to second-guess everything. Why didn't he divorce her when he caught her with the gardener? Why had he married her to begin with? He did not realize what an evil monster she was. He racked his brain and could find no way out of it. He knew she was right; he would lose everything in a divorce. How would he take care of Marina and Maddie then? He buried his head in his hands and closed his eyes. His life had become a nightmare.

His heart wanted nothing more than Marina and Maddie. Ellen's heart wanted nothing more than money and self-satisfaction. He knew he had to find a way out of the situation, but she seemed to have blocked him at every pass. Every pass except perhaps one.

He sent a text to Mac. "Emergency, have Jacob come by house at earliest convenience. No phone calls." He hit send and then erased it immediately. She would probably be able to get her hands on the actual text if she wanted to, but she would not know about it right away. He hoped fervently that Jacob had a solution for him. He had proven repeatedly to be the ace in Kevin's pocket, but this time, there was no alternative.

Later that afternoon, Jacob walked into Kevin's office and found him sitting looking out the window at his garden.

"What's going on, Kevin?" he asked right away. Kevin lifted his finger to his lips and waved his hand for Jacob to follow him. They walked silently out the back door of the kitchen and Kevin quietly asked Sarah, his housekeeper, to keep it to herself that she had seen the two of them walking together. She nodded and smiled at him.

They walked down the gardener's path to the beach and then walked away from the property. They were a good distance down the beach before Kevin spoke and told Jacob what had happened. Jacob shook his head and rubbed his hand over his chin.

"I never did like that bitch," he stated flatly.

"Jake, please tell me you have something we can do about this." He hoped against hope, his breath frozen in his chest while he waited.

Jacob thought carefully and said, "So you say she was screwing the gardener in her room, right?"

Kevin closed his eyes a moment and tried to get the image of it out of his mind. "Yes."

"Do you think she'd have another fling in there?" he asked with a gleam in his eye.

"It's possible. She said she was going to have her boyfriends back here at the house, anytime and anywhere she wanted them," he said with a guttural disgust.

"Good," Jacob said with a big smile. "We may be able to get you out of this. See, one of the things I insisted on before I let you marry her was to have her sign a prenuptial agreement."

Kevin blinked and looked at him in surprise. "I didn't know that. She signed a pre-nup? I told you we didn't need one."

Jacob chuckled at him. "Yeah, I know you did, buddy. The trouble is, I have seen things go poorly for too many men. I told her that she could not have access to all your money during the marriage unless she signed the pre-nup first. I spit out a lot of legal jargon and confused her and she panicked and signed the damn thing. Thank god. That pre-nup says that if she is ever unfaithful to you, she gets nothing if you two get divorced; not a single dime."

Kevin stared at him in utter amazement. "I had no idea about that!"

"I know. It is alright. Listen. This is a little underhanded, but we can make it work. I have friends in the film industry. We call your little woman down to your office, and when she sits down with us, we offer her a settlement. A lump sum one-time monetary amount to divorce you, leave and never say a word about anything. If she takes it, we are all set. She probably won't take it, but that is alright, because while she's down in the office with the two of us, I will have an installation person up in her bedroom installing hidden cameras. We record her until we have some footage of her indulging in extra marital relations and then we have the upper hand. You can divorce her without worrying about paying her a single dime. She signed it; it's a done deal. Also, she doesn't have much room to complain about you having an in vitro child if she was out having an affair."

Kevin felt awful and good about it, volleying between the two emotions.

"I have to ask you this, though, buddy. Have you and Marina… uh… have you been more than friends at any point?" he looked at his friend with slight concern.

Kevin shook his head. "No. I kissed her today, but that was it. That was the first time and it's the only thing that's happened between us."

Jacob looked at his friend with some pity. "Do you love her?"

Kevin sighed and nodded his head. "I do. Jacob, I love that woman so much. I wish I could spend every day of the rest of my life with her and help her raise Maddie as her husband. She's amazing."

Jacob nodded and smiled. "Does she love you?"

"Yeah, she said she does. She said she has been really struggling with it because of my marriage. She didn't want to get in the way of my commitment to Ellen." Kevin rolled his eyes at the irony.

"And you two haven't done anything more than kiss today, right?" Jacob double-checked.

Kevin nodded. "That's right. I want to do more, and so does she, but we are keeping this on the straight and narrow."

"Would she testify to that if I needed her to?" Jacob asked.

Kevin looked at him seriously, "Yes, but I don't want her dragged into this. This looks like it's going to get ugly and she really does not need any of that. Let's keep her out of it, please? Can we do that?"

Jacob waved his hand. "Don't worry about it. I doubt we'll need her. What we need to do is get this plan in gear. It is not going to be easy for you to be underhanded.

"I know how you are, all morals and no risk. You have to commit to this fully or it won't work. Are you in?" he asked, looking at Kevin, knowing he was asking a great deal from a man who prided himself on honor.

"I'm in," Kevin said solemnly.

Jacob grinned and pulled his phone from his pocket, dialing a number and speaking to someone for a short period before hanging up and looking at Kevin with a wide smile.

"He's on his way. We have a camera installer. Let's do this thing."

"Now?" Kevin asked in utter surprise.

"Right now. I want that bitch out of your house," Jacob said staunchly and turned to walk back up the beach. Kevin just chuckled a little, shook his head and followed his friend back up to the house. He trusted Jacob completely, and he knew that no matter how ugly it got, his friend was going to help him through it and protect him the entire time.

They were sitting in Kevin's office two hours later with newly printed paperwork ready for their meeting when Ellen breezed through the door and scowled at Jacob who finished a text on his phone and then looked up at her.

"I told you not to involve anyone in our situation!" she snapped menacingly at Kevin.

"And what situation would that be?" Jacob asked, looking at her with piercing eyes and a killer stare.

She narrowed her gaze at him. "None of your damn business," she almost growled at him. "What do you want?" she asked, standing over him with her hands on her hips.

"Why don't you have a seat?" Jacob asked, indicating the sofa opposite him.

"I'm busy and I don't have time for you." She said it coolly, peering down her nose at him.

He looked at her in all seriousness. "You have time for this. *Now sit down.*"

She plopped down on the sofa and tilted her head at him. "So what's so important?"

"Kevin wants to make you a very lucrative one time offer," he said, leaning forward and placing a sheet of paper on the table.

She looked down at it and then back up at Jacob, not having taken the time to read anything on the paper he put in front of her. "An offer for what?" she asked, sliding her gaze sharply to Kevin and then returning it to Jacob.

"Kevin wants an immediate divorce, and he is willing to overlook your marital indiscretions and offer you a single lump sum settlement in return for a quick and amicable divorce. You sign the page, you get the generous settlement money he has offered you, and you go your separate ways. You never talk about Kevin again, publicly or otherwise. Ever." Jacob never took his steely eyes off hers.

She scoffed. "And why would I do something stupid like that?" she asked haughtily.

Jacob sneered at her like a shark circling its prey. "Because if you don't sign this paper right now then you waive all monies that might be gotten by you in the future during this divorce. You see, my dear, it is going to happen. Your farce of a marriage is over. The question is whether or not you will walk away from it with anything at all.

"You see, Ellen, I think you have an affinity for Kevin's money, so as a kind gesture on his part, he is willing to let you have some of it when you leave, if you leave now and if you leave quietly. If you choose to argue and fight this out, you are going to walk away with exactly what you came into this farce of a marriage with; nothing at all. Not two thin dimes to rub together. Am I making myself clear enough for you?"

Ellen laughed at him and leaned back against the sofa. "Well, honey, I know you were part of Kevin's little escapade in having that bastard kid outside of our marriage. I do not have to bluff you or try to scare you, but the fact is, I know everything about what happened, and I know he has been seeing her on the side. No judge is going to have any sympathy for a guy who is having kids outside of his marriage.

"I will wind up walking away with all of it, the house, the money, the cars and boats, his business… everything. All of it will be mine. I already warned Kevin about this, and I told him not to involve you, but here you two are, about to screw up royally. I will take you down so far, Kevin, that you never see the light of day again."

Jacob leaned forward and stared her down. "Oh, I don't think so, you see, there's so much more to this than you know. If you have a brain cell left in that little head of yours, you will sign this right now, take the money and run. Kevin hopes you will, but myself, well, I think you're not smart enough to know when to quit, and to be honest, I really hope you don't sign it, because I would love to see what happens to you next."

She wavered slightly; it rippled over her face for the briefest moment, and both men saw it, but she poked her chin out and shook her head. "No way. There's no way you can win against me."

Jacob's phone went off and he looked at the text message on it and then looked up at Ellen. "Your call. Sign it right now or walk out and you get nothing, and possibly more trouble than you could ever imagine."

She stood up and put her hands on her hips. "Go to hell. Both of you." With that, she walked out of the office and Jacob leaned back and grinned.

"What's that look for?" Kevin asked suspiciously.

"Oh… we're all set for a good long, recorded look at her bedroom. Now all we have to do is let her do what she wants to, and she will hang herself." He stood up and clapped Kevin on the back. "Give it a week, brother, let her hang herself. I will be in touch. Stay out of her room, and leave her alone."

He turned and walked toward the office door. "Oh… and uh, you'll be seeing some new employees around here. Gardeners, pool boys, handymen… leave them alone and stay in your office. You got that?" Jacob grinned.

Kevin sighed and nodded. "Yes, boss." Then Jacob disappeared and not two hours later, Kevin began to see new help around the yard and the house. Young, strong, beautiful men who could have been models or Chippendale dancers, and all of them were working hard in the hot sun wearing just barely essential clothing.

A week passed and he did not text Marina, and she did not text him. She was waiting for him to make up his mind about whom and what he wanted, and he was aching for her with every fiber of his being. He didn't want to jeopardize Jacob's plan or give Ellen any kind of edge, so he worked from his office.

He stayed in his office and in his room and now and again he would see the beautiful young men around the yard or the house, and he would see them coming and going from Ellen's bedroom. She made a blatant point of making out with one of them in her doorway one morning when Kevin was leaving his room to go to the office.

As he passed them, silently looking the other way, he heard the young man ask Ellen who he was, and she replied, "Oh, he's no one. He is just a guy who's living here for a short period of time. He'll be gone soon." Then she kissed him and pulled him back into her bedroom, closing the door behind her.

Another week went by and Kevin thought he was going to go crazy trying to wait for Jacob's plan to be at a point where he could contact Marina. Jacob and Mac had both sent her messages, promising her that everything was alright, that Kevin would be in touch with her as soon as he could. They were unable to tell her anything else because they didn't want to give her any information that Ellen could use against him later.

Kevin tried to avoid Ellen, but she became more blatant about her affairs as if she were rubbing them each in Kevin's face for the fun of it. She had sex with one young man in the pool and was so loud about it that Kevin and the house staff had to close the windows and doors. She had sex with another man on the rug in front of the fireplace in the living room and with yet a different young gardener, not far from Kevin's office.

It made him nauseated but he no longer felt the pain of a broken heart. He was solely biding his time until she was gone, waiting impatiently for the day that he could talk to Marina again without concern of repercussions from his contact with her.

The third week passed and Ellen went from being a cold-hearted tramp to a raging bitch. She had men in and out of her room constantly, and she was growing short tempered and irritable on the rare occasions that Kevin saw her. She had begun throwing things at him again and lashing out at him in emotional bursts, and her appetite for men somehow increased, though Kevin didn't think it at all possible.

Jacob finally came back to the house and was almost gleeful in his demeanor. Kevin sat with him and they talked in his office for a long time before Jacob finally asked him to call Ellen in to meet with them. She took her time about it, as they expected she probably would and she eventually sauntered in looking a bit pale and very angry and then took a seat when Jacob bid her to do so.

She looked up at him and snapped, "So what the hell do you want?"

He sat on the sofa opposite her and grinned at her.

"What are you grinning about?" she yelled at him, losing her temper quickly.

"Well, you remember the last time I sat you down in here and told you to sign that paper so you could walk away with some money or you were going to regret it?" he asked in a chipper tone.

"Yeah?" she shot back disinterestedly.

He picked up a remote control and pressed one of the buttons. The wooden cabinet over the bar opened and a flat screen monitor moved out slightly toward them.

"Kevin here, under my direction, felt that the security in this home was severely under-managed, so we had some security cameras installed to make sure that things around the house were protected and alright, and that everyone was safe. Boy, were we surprised to find out that you've had all kinds of fun, all over this house, with all the staff your husband has hired on. Let's have a look shall we?" he said, still somewhere between gleeful and giddy.

He pressed play and as the video showed her in her bed with several different men over a long period of time, she went from shock to fury and screamed at Jacob.

"How could you? You bastard! That's my bedroom! My private space! How dare you put cameras in there! I want those videos right now, all of them!" she lunged for him, but he moved and she missed him.

"Oh now... don't get ahead of me here, honey. You see, I have you on tape with no less than... uh, how many was it, Kevin?" he asked with a grin, knowing full well how many it was.

Kevin rubbed his finger over his chin and looked through a stack of papers on his desk. "Sixteen."

Jacob's mouth fell open in mock surprise. "Sixteen? My word! Are you sure? Sixteen? Really?"

Kevin raised his eyebrows and nodded and Ellen glared at them in sheer horror. "It's true. Sixteen."

Jacob continued. "Right, so we have you on tape with about sixteen different men, having illicit affairs with each and every one of them, right here under your poor devoted husband's nose, in the home that you both share, and so we'd like to ask you again to sign the divorce papers, except this time, you don't get a dime. Not one single red cent."

She shrieked. "You can't do that! I will too get every single bit of it!"

Jacob shook his head and smiled broadly at her. "Oh no, honey. You can't. You see, back when you first tricked Kevin into getting engaged to you, I had you sign a different little piece of paper. Do you remember that one? Before you married him? It was called a prenuptial agreement. What it says, and what you agreed to, is that if you are ever unfaithful to him and he divorces you, you will lose everything and have to walk away from the marriage without any profit whatsoever.

"You get to take away what you came into the marriage with in the beginning, which was, if I recall, nothing. We have you on film cheating on your husband several times with more than sixteen different men. That means you get nothing in the divorce."

She stood up, screamed at them both, and began to cry. "I'm not signing it! There's not going to be a divorce!"

Jacob stood up, walked over to her, and held out a pen for her. "You will sign it, or I will publish all those videos for purchase worldwide in stores and on the Internet, which will earn you a whole new reputation, and me a pretty good chunk of money."

She grabbed the pen from Jacob's hand and threw it. "You're a bastard! Both of you! You are horrible bastards! I cannot believe this! How could you do this to me?" She turned and faced Kevin, crying and screaming at him. "How could you do this to your own wife? I thought you were honorable and respectful! I thought you lived by some great moral code! What happened to that?" she sobbed at him.

He shook his head at her. "I could ask you the same thing. I have broken no code. I have not cheated on you, I have not gone against a single vow I made to you at our wedding, and you have broken all of them. You have no right, no place to be angry with me. None whatsoever."

She stomped around his desk and clenched her fists, raging at him. "I have every right to be angry with you! You went out and had a child with another woman! What the hell does that say about our marriage? What kind of way is that to treat your wife? You sneaked behind my back and had a child! You never said one word to me about what you were doing!" she screamed at him and then collapsed on the sofa in a fountain of tears.

Both men looked at her and shook their heads waiting for her to calm down. She finally sat up, red faced and puffy eyed, and laughed. Kevin raised one eyebrow.

"What's funny?" he asked suspiciously.

She giggled and then stood up and walked out of the room and Jacob and Kevin stared at each other in silence for a moment.

"What's she doing?" Jacob asked.

"I have no idea, but whatever it is, it can't be good. She has really been on edge lately, so there is no telling what she is has been doing She's been completely unpredictable," Kevin told him.

Minutes later, she stomped back into the room and slammed the door behind her.

"You two think you are so smart. Well, you are not. You aren't smart enough to get one past this lady. You think you are going to smear me all over with sex tapes, but if you do, you are just going to be hurting Kevin. Mister 'I am Going To Have a Baby With Someone Else'.

"Well, I've got a surprise for the two of you. I am not signing any divorce papers. I am not leaving this house. I'm going to have everything handed to me on a silver platter, because I'm pregnant with Kevin's kid."

She laughed through her angry tears at them and slammed a piece of paper down on the desk in front of Kevin, then walked over to the sofa she had been sitting and crying on and plopped down on it, her Cheshire Cat grin spread over her tear stained face.

Jacob and Kevin were both in complete shock. "What do you mean you're pregnant?" Kevin asked in amazement. "That's not possible! You had a hysterectomy!"

She laughed wildly again and shook her head. "No I didn't. I just lied to you and said that because I did not want to have a kid with you and now look at me. I'm knocked up and it couldn't have happened at a better time."

Kevin felt his heart crash from his chest to the floor. "You lied to me? You never had a hysterectomy?"

"Look who's finally coming around," she sneered at him. "Yeah, I lied to you. I lie to you all the time about everything so I can get what I want. I told you I loved you, and I never did. I told you I wanted to fix this damn marriage and go on a second honeymoon so I could keep you and stay all cozy in your deep pockets, and I actually slept with you for what, the first time in more than a year and look what happens to me.

"I am knocked up with your damn kid. Luckily, this kid is going to ensure that I get everything I have coming to me, and neither one of you jackasses is going to keep me from getting it. This kid is my guarantee to all the money, no matter how many sex tapes you have. I am not signing the divorce papers, and I am not leaving this house. Me and this kid are going to stay here forever."

Jacob shook his head. "It's not possible. Even if you did lie to him about the hysterectomy, you two haven't had sex in well over a year and you have screwed dozens of men over the last few months!"

Kevin sank down into his chair as he held the paper in his hand and read it. Jacob looked at him with laser beam intensity.

"What does it say?" he asked.

"It says she is pregnant and that she got pregnant when we went to Hawaii on our second honeymoon," Kevin said, feeling almost robotic when he said it. He felt like his soul had been blown completely out of his body. He could not think or move and could only barely breathe. He had no idea what he was going to do about this situation.

Ellen just sat on the sofa and laughed at him wickedly.

Jacob's gaze shot back to her. "Don't you laugh, you crazy bitch. You are going to lose that baby the minute it is born. You are an unfit mother. I'm not letting this go. You are still going to be out of here as soon as I can get you out. You will see! You are gone!" he hollered at her.

She stood up and walked past him with a smirk on her face. "The only place I'm leaving is this office. Now get rid of all those sex tapes. You don't want your poor wife and the mother of your next child to look like a tramp in front of the press, do you? No? I didn't think so. I'll be upstairs. I have a date."

She turned once more and looked down her nose at them both. "Get those damn cameras the hell out of this house, too, I'm not a peep show." Then she slammed the door and they both sat back in silence and looked at each other.

"What on earth am I going to do now?" Kevin asked.

"I know you think the timing makes that kid yours, and who knows, maybe it is your baby, but I still want a paternity test done on the baby, and no matter what, she is out of here. We can sue for custody of the baby and kick her out. No judge is going to give a baby to a mother with her trashy tramp record. She just left to go lay down with another guy! Minutes after telling you she was having your child.

"She won't be here long. Don't worry about it. You are still getting a divorce, you are still going to be able to be with Marina and Maddie, and she is still going to be gone. We just have to figure this out. Give me a little time to work on it, and let's have a drink." He stood up and poured them both a shot of whiskey.

Kevin shook his head and looked into the bottom of his glass. She was pregnant. She had lied to him about the hysterectomy. The whole reason, in fact the only reason that he had gone looking for a mother for his child outside of his marriage, was because Ellen said she couldn't have children, and it was a lie, and now she was pregnant. He was blown away by the idea of it.

He did consider that the one single good thing that came of it, or rather, the two best things were that he would not have met Marina if Ellen had not lied to him, and he would not have Maddie, and those two girls were the most important people in his life.

"I'm grateful to have you here to help me, Jacob," Kevin said, lifting his tumbler in a toast to his friend. "Thank you for helping me through this."

Jacob grumbled and lifted his glass, tipping it slightly toward Kevin. "That bitch is going down. I will find every way I can to make sure it happens. You do not deserve this, Kevin, you really don't. You deserve to be happy with Marina and Maddie, and I'm going to do my best to make sure that happens."

Kevin nodded. "I hope so. Jacob, I have to tell you, I feel like my whole life depends on it."

Chapter 7

Kevin felt as though he could not be tied up in more knots. His wife was pregnant, after having first told him that she had a hysterectomy and could not have children, and then admitting to him that she had lied to him about the medical procedure only because she didn't want children with him.

Because of her lie, he had gone outside of their marriage and found another woman who agreed to conceive and carry his child through in vitro fertilization. He had fallen in love with the in vitro mother of his child, Marina, while she was still pregnant with their daughter, and more than anything, he wanted to marry her and raise their baby girl, Maddie, together.

Kevin was a man ruled by morality and extremely high values, and because he was married to Ellen, he would not consider cheating on her with Marina, and he had committed himself to reconstructing the broken marriage that he and Ellen found themselves.

Ellen was having constant affairs with men outside of her marriage to Kevin and completely abstaining from her marriage bed. She had spent two weeks with Kevin in Hawaii and during that time, she had finally made love with her husband. Now, a month later, she had discovered that she was pregnant, claiming that the father of her child was Kevin, stopping him from divorcing her just as he had made up his mind to take that step so he could be with Marina and Maddie.

It was a tangled web, indeed. Marina had fallen in love with Kevin, and had recently admitted it to him, and while she struggled with her love for a married man and the father of her child, her ex-fiancé Lamar had returned, deeply remorseful of having left her at the altar and determined to win her back and become her husband and Maddie's step-father.

Marina wanted Kevin desperately, but she also knew that it wasn't right to go after a married man, and she realized that her chances of him getting a divorce and marrying her were pretty slim. She knew what she wanted, but she knew she probably couldn't have it, and that left her with the choice of either being alone or allowing Lamar the chance to love her again.

Kevin had his car pick Marina and Maddie up at their house and he took them to the boardwalk for the day to enjoy the sunshine and to spend time with the woman he loved and his beautiful baby girl.

He lavished his love on them, being careful to keep his closeness to Marina as simple as possible, so that he wouldn't hurt her. He had asked her for time to make a decision about whether or not he would be getting a divorce and leaving his wife for her, or stay with his wife and keep their relationship a platonic arrangement.
Marina had been waiting patiently and quietly, and it had been more than a week. As they walked down the boardwalk together, she felt it was time to bring it up to Kevin again.

"I know I said I would be patient and wait for you to make up your mind, and I have been, but being out with you like this today, like a family, it makes me want your answer. Have you thought anymore about it? Have you decided about divorcing your wife?" Marina asked, as her heart pounded nervously in her chest.

Kevin had known that it would come up. He felt horrible about making her wait for such an important answer. He had gone over and over the conversation in his head, trying to decide if he would tell her that Ellen was pregnant, trying to decide if he would let her carry the pain and burden of that news.

He had finally decided against it. It was not something he wanted her to worry about unless it was confirmed that he was the father of Ellen's baby and then he would have to stay with her. She was his wife, and if she was pregnant with his child, he would not break his home to be with the woman he loved and wanted more than anything. He had made a commitment to Ellen at their wedding, with the intention of having a family with her and it looked as though that was exactly what was happening.

He sighed. "Marina, I know you want an answer, and I wish I could give you one right now. I wish I had the right words to say the outcome that we are both hoping for, and that is to be together." He stopped walking and turned to look at her, placing his hand on her cheek. "I want you more than anything in this world. I love you so very much, but I cannot make a choice about what can happen with us right now."

She blinked back the tears that stung her eyes and swallowed the sadness that choked her. "Why not? Shouldn't it be simple? Shouldn't it be easy to choose the woman you love?"

He gazed at her, looking into her blue-gray eyes and losing himself in them for a long moment. How he wished he could be with her and keep her at his side for the rest of his life.

"Marina, I wish it was that simple, but it really isn't. There have been some developments with Ellen. There are some legal issues that have complicated my ability to make an immediate choice. You and Maddie are my only real happiness and I want to be with you both, all the time, but the problems with Ellen have gotten out of hand and it is much more complicated than me just choosing between the two of you. There's a great deal at stake, much more than money, and it will be a little while before I know what my real options are; what I can do and how it will affect everyone involved in this."

He leaned toward her and pressed his lips gently to her forehead, pulling her close to him and holding her against him for a moment. They closed their eyes and they breathed each other in, then he let her go and looked down at her.

"Please give me a little more time. I am so sorry to have to ask you to be patient and wait, but I'm afraid that is exactly what I need to do. Could you please find it in your heart to wait just a little while longer and give me just a little more time? I hate making you wait, but there's really nothing that I can do just yet. Please?" he asked softly, running his fingers down the side of her beautiful face.

She felt as though her heart was being pulled apart and it was almost more than she could bear. She closed her eyes for a moment and breathed in, soothing herself and calming the waves of emotion that crashed through her. She could give him more time. She was in no hurry to be in a relationship. She was focused on herself and Maddie and making sure that she gave Maddie a good start, but she didn't want to be stuck in limbo forever, either.

Kevin waited nervously for her answer. He hoped she understood how much she meant to him and how much he truly wanted her, but he could not give her a decision until he knew for certain what was happening with Ellen.

She opened her eyes and looked up at him. "I'll wait. I want to be with you, I want to raise Maddie with you as a family, but I understand that there is a lot going on for you right now and I can wait a little longer. Please don't make me wait too long, though, Kevin. I can't sit on a shelf and hope you choose me someday. If you aren't going to be with me, then let me know soon so that I can try to fall out of love with you and get on with raising my daughter as your friend."

Her honesty cut at him and he closed his arms around her tightly and embraced her. He wanted to beg her not to try to get over him, to stay in love with him and be his forever. He couldn't stand the idea of her being with another man, but he also couldn't promise her that he would be able to be hers.

"Thank you for giving me more time. I'll try to get it sorted out as quickly as I can." He kissed her warm cheek. She closed her eyes as his lips touched her skin and wished with all of her heart that he could be that close and even closer to her every day of her life.

They turned and strolled down the boardwalk, hearts heavy but glad to be together. They spent the better part of the day talking and laughing, playing with their baby girl and enjoying the warm sun and fresh sea air. It was a rare day that they were both very glad to spend together.

After Kevin returned Marina and Maddie to her house and hugged them both goodbye, kissing their cheeks as he left, he headed back to his own home, sorry to be going there. He walked up the rounded staircase to Ellen's room and opened the door to find that she wasn't there. He searched all of the upstairs and went downstairs to look for her. She was nowhere to be seen.

He knew she was home. Her new Lamborghini was in the garage. He walked out behind the house and stood beside the pool, looking around the gardens. There was no sign of her, but after a few moments, he could hear voices and he walked toward the sound. He realized what he was hearing before he got to the source of it, and it turned his stomach and steeled his body.

He walked into the maintenance room at the back of the pool house. The door was open. He stepped onto the concrete floor and slid his hands into his pockets, looking with disgust upon the scene of his wife with her clothing half peeled off and pushed aside. She was bent over a work table as the newly hired model-beautiful pool man stood behind her, his hands grasping her breasts, his pants dropped down to his knees, and his hips grinding into Ellen's. They were both in the throes of pleasure, gasping and groaning loudly.

Kevin cleared his throat and raised his voice. "Ellen!"

She turned and looked over her shoulder at him and gave him an extremely annoyed and intolerant look. The pool man looked horrified as he turned to see Kevin, but Ellen reached her hands around herself to grab onto his hips and hold him inside of her. "Don't stop, Jose, it's no one we need to worry about."

Kevin sighed. "When you have a minute, please come to my office, Ellen." He looked at them both and shook his head, then turned on his heel and walked out. He didn't think he would ever be used to seeing her in intimate situations with other men. But because of the cameras around the house and their non-existent relationship with each other that resulted in a complete lack of respect toward Kevin, he had seen quite a bit of it, both in person and on video. It no longer surprised him, though it disgusted him immensely.

He strode into his office and poured himself a drink. Then he sat at his desk to work until she came in. He focused on everything in the moment, rather than letting himself think about what she was doing outside in the pool maintenance room with the pool man.

He hadn't fired any of the staff that Ellen had been having sexual flings with on Jacob's orders, because Jacob was building a case. There were four men on payroll and under his employment, that he was aware of, that were screwing his wife all over his property and his house, and Jacob had insisted that he left her to it, saying that he was giving her just enough rope to hang herself.

It was Jacob who saw to the hiring of the new male staff, and it hadn't escaped Kevin's attention, or Ellen's, that all of them were extraordinarily fit and stunningly handsome. It didn't take her any time at all to get the four he knew about into her bed or her body, and it was something she indulged in frequently.

Forty-five minutes later, she sauntered into his office in a string bikini that barely covered her beautifully sculpted body. Her long sable brown hair was hanging loosely around her shoulders and her dark eyes were sharp and fierce. She sat down on one of the couches and waved at the couch opposite her.

"Come sit over here if you want to talk with me. I don't like sitting at the desk with you; it makes me feel inferior to you, and I'm not." She spoke in an even tone.

Kevin watched her for a moment and then stood up and walked to the couch she pointed at and sat opposite her.

"Can I offer you a beverage?" he asked.

She laughed at him and shook her head. "Always so polite. I'll have whatever you're drinking." She answered dryly.

He stared at her. "I'm drinking whiskey. May I get you something else?"

She scoffed. "Water is fine."

Kevin frowned at her. "You aren't drinking alcohol while you're pregnant, are you, Ellen?"

She shook her head. "Not a chance. I'm staying healthy." She patted her stomach. "I have to take care of this little cash cow." She had made a point of telling Kevin that she expected to be treated like a queen since she was having his child, and that she wouldn't be getting a divorce from him because he was now locked into their marriage as a result of the baby in her belly.

He wiped his finger over his brow and looked at her. "That's something I want to talk with you about."

She narrowed her eyes at him. "What is it?"

He handed her an ice water and looked at her earnestly. "Your frequent trysts are a danger to the baby, and I want you to stop having intercourse."

She gaped at him. "You think you can control me? You can't! I can do whatever I want to do, and it's not your business what I do!" she hissed at him.

Kevin kept his tone level. "I mean it, Ellen, you could hurt the child. Besides, it may have completely escaped your attention, but we are in fact married, and you should not be having sex with the staff all over the house we share."

She leaned forward and glared at him. "I'll do whatever I want to, Kevin dear, and you can keep your opinions to yourself. If I want to take a lover now and then, I will, because I need the affection. You and I aren't intimate, so what other choice do I have?"

He held his tongue in check and was silent a moment before answering her. "You have several choices. I don't sleep with anyone else. I don't have extra marital affairs or sex with other women in our home or anywhere else for that matter! Perhaps you could show a little restraint when you are in our home and act like you are actually married!"

"Oh no, Kevin, you aren't out sleeping with other women, you're out having children with them! You didn't just go out and find some woman to have an affair with, no; you went out and started a family with another woman! That's far worse than me getting a little love in my lonely life!" she snapped angrily at him.

Ire rose in him. "I only found a surrogate mother because you told me you had a hysterectomy after we were married! You spent all of that time before we were married telling me how much you wanted to start a family with me and how anxious you were to have children.

"Once we were married, you left our marriage bed and hibernated in your own room. You almost never made love with me. When I brought up having children, you would push the idea off and when I pressed the issue again, you told me you had the hysterectomy, and then you told me to go have a child on my own! It was your idea." He paused and took a gulp of his whiskey.

"I never would have even thought of it if you hadn't come up with the idea for me. So I did… I listened to you and I went to find a woman to have a child for me, but I didn't sleep with her, it was an in vitro fertilization and you know that full well. You're the one who sneaked into my office and read through her file!"

"I wouldn't have had to sneak if you had been honest with me right from the beginning and told me what you were doing!" she fired back at him.

"Nothing in this office is your business!" He stated that firmly. "You are very well taken care of, you lack for nothing, I am completely dedicated to you, and you have no reason to go snooping in here!" He closed his eyes and took a deep breath. "I was saying, you told me you'd had a hysterectomy and then you tell me almost a year later that you lied to me, that not only is it possible for you to have children, but that you are pregnant with my child! I wouldn't have believed you if I hadn't seen the paperwork from the doctor!"

Her foul look turned into an evil grin. "I knew you wouldn't believe me. That's why I got the medical confirmation. Now I can stay forever, and you will always have to take care of me." She smirked. "I'm never going to divorce you."

He watched her for a long moment. "Then you had better stop sleeping with the staff and any other lovers I'm unaware of, and I mean immediately."

She narrowed her eyes at him, "I will have lovers as long as I want to. Someone has to give me affection. Now, if you want to start talking about sacrifices, I would be willing to make a trade. I'll stop seeing my boys if you stop seeing that woman and her kid. I mean completely. No visits, no phone calls, no messaging; nothing. No contact whatsoever. You stop seeing them and I will stop having fun with the guys." She smirked coolly at him.

He felt embers of anger burning brightly in him. "You can't ask me to do that! That's my daughter you're trying to keep me from! There's absolutely no way I'm going to stop spending time with my daughter. None. That won't happen!" he raised his voice.

She shrugged and shook her head. "Well then, don't ask me to quit. I'll do what I want to. You can't control me any more than I can control you, so we are either going to have to make a truce, and that was my offer to you for a truce, or you can just let it go and forget about it, because nobody tells me what to do."

He knew there was only one other reason she might listen to. "What about the baby's health? If it's so important for you to have this baby to stay in this marriage, then why would you jeopardize the health of the little one you are carrying by having intercourse with so many different men?"

She just shook her head at him. "Don't pull that on me. I'm taking care of myself and this baby, and the two of us are going to be around here for the rest of your life." She curled the corners of her red lips up into a Cheshire cat smile and then stood up and walked out of the room.

He felt drowned in defeat. He hadn't meant to fight with her, and it had gotten ugly between them again. He had only wanted to talk with her about curbing or stopping her extramarital affairs. He was worried about the baby, worried about her health and he hated seeing her with other men.

Kevin couldn't believe she had offered to stop sleeping around in return for his abandoning Maddie and Marina. There was no way he could do that. He had given his word that he would always be there to take care of them, and he wasn't about to go back on his word or the contractual agreement that he had with Marina.

He leaned back against the couch and tilted his head back until he was looking at the ceiling. He stared without looking at the painted fresco on the ceiling. He loved Marina and he wanted her more than anything. They had a daughter together, and he had never done more than kiss her once. He was married to a woman who practically hated him, who had a seemingly endless hunger for any number of other men, and she was pregnant.

He could not begin to see how to sort it out and make the right choices for the most people involved, including himself. He knew he would have to make some choices soon, though, because Marina was not going to sit idly by and wait for him as he continued to put off answering her desire to be with him.

Chapter 8

Lamar knocked on Marina's front door and she called out for him to come in. He had been coming to visit her every day. She walked out to the living room and saw that he had a large bouquet of fresh flowers in his hand and a wide smile on his face.

"Good morning," she said, walking toward him.

"Good morning, beautiful." He hugged her and kissed her cheek gently. He held the bouquet out to her and she looked at it with consternation and then looked up at him.

"Lamar, you don't need to keep bringing me things. It feels like it's out of hand. You bring things all the time. Flowers, chocolate, books, breakfast, coffee and tea… I appreciate your thoughtfulness, but it feels like you are trying to buy my friendship back and that's not necessary. It's really not. You and I, we are alright now. We're in a better place now. It's okay. You shouldn't be bringing me things all the time." Her eyes shone with earnest concern.

He spread his hands wide and laughed a little, "What? I just like bringing you things. Can't I spoil you a little? You love flowers, chocolate, and books… all the things I bring you. I love to see you smile. You should be spoiled. I don't mind doing it." He reached for her hand and pulled her toward him slowly, "There's nothing that's too good for you. These are just little tokens of my affection for you, that's all. Just friendly little gifts." He slid his arms around her waist and drew her up to him in an embrace, holding her so that he could still look down into her eyes.

She felt the all too familiar flutter of butterflies that began to zoom around her stomach and heart. Lamar had been seeing her nearly every day, coming over to her house and spending time with her and Maddie. He had continued to become physically closer to her, and while her heart was caught up in Kevin, her body remembered her former fiancé and lover very well, and much to her chagrin, it reacted warmly to Lamar's touch and attention.

"Well, you do too much. I don't want to feel obligated to you, and you showering me with gifts like this tends to make me feel like I need to do something in return for you, as well. Please don't do that. Please stop bringing me things," she asked, looking up at him.

He gazed down into her blue-gray eyes for a long moment and then slowly leaned his lips down to press them softly against her forehead.

"Whatever you want, my girl. I meant to make you happy, not to make you feel bad. I'm sorry. I'll make it up to you." He spoke quietly, lowering his face to her cheek and brushing his lips over her skin there. His warm breath made her tingle and she drew a deep breath and turned her head away from him, looking down.

"I'd better get back into the kitchen. I'm right in the middle of baking cookies. I need to see to them." She placed her hands on the solid wall of his chest and gave a little push, and he let her go, watching her as she turned and walked back into the kitchen. He followed her and stopped at the little bouncer on the counter where Maddie was laying, looking around at them both.

"She just gets bigger every day. She's so beautiful." He walked up behind Marina as she faced the counter and mixed her cookie dough. Lamar slid his hands around her waist and leaned his head onto her shoulder, speaking softly into her ear.

"What do you think our children would look like, if we had them?" he asked.

"I guess they'd be beautiful, too, but now we won't know."

He moved his hands up to her shoulders and began to massage her lightly. "I thought we could go to the park today and have a picnic. Get Maddie out in the sun. What do you think? It's a really nice day."

She began to spoon the dough onto the cookie sheet before her. "I think that would be nice. Are you sure you have time?"

"I always have time for you two," Lamar said with a smile. He let his hands fall from Marina and walked over to Maddie to play with her while Marina finished filling the cookie sheet and put it in the oven.

Half an hour later, they were walking down the sidewalk pushing Maddie's stroller and heading toward the park. Lamar brought lunch for them as well as the flowers he'd given Marina. They set up a blanket underneath a tree beside the small lake and Marina laid Maddie out on her back.

Lamar and Marina ate lunch and fresh baked cookies, and spent a while playing with the baby. He reached out to her, touching her hand, her arm, or her shoulder when he spoke to her, or when he handed her something or fed her a bite. His close proximity did not escape her notice. She felt comfortable with him, but she realized he was trying to gently push away the grey boundaries between them.

Partway through the afternoon, Marina's phone rang and she answered it saying, "Hi, you!" as a grin spread over her face and Lamar looked on in suspicion.

"We're good. We're at the park having a picnic." Then she laughed. "No, she ate before we came. We miss you, too. Oh, that would be nice! Yeah, we should be back at the house in a while. Dinner? Sure! We'll see you tonight. I love you, too."

She hung up and then looked up at Lamar to see him frowning slightly.

"Who was that?" he asked.

She bit her lower lip and then answered, "That was Kevin."

Lamar looked away and sighed and Marina stood up and began to pack their things. "I think we should head back to the house. Maddie will need her nap soon."

He helped her pack and they walked back. He pushed the stroller and she walked beside him. They remarked upon the houses and gardens they passed and when they reached Marina's house, she took Maddie into her bedroom and laid her in her bassinet.

Lamar followed her into her room and when she turned to leave Maddie, she found herself facing him.

She looked up at him and he gazed down into her eyes. Her breath caught in her chest as he reached his hand up and touched her cheek, running his fingers over it. Marina reached her hand up to cover his, holding his hand still for a moment before he moved his thumb over her lower lip and she felt warm electricity spreading through her.

"Lamar…" she whispered, wondering how to help him see that this wasn't the best idea for them. He made use of the pause in her thoughts to lean down to her and press his lips lightly to hers. She gasped and he wrapped his arms around her and pulled her to him, his hands firm on her.

He moved his mouth over hers softly, warmly, as he held her, and she felt confusion and heat begin to swirl through her. Her breath caught and he opened her mouth with his, tasting her tentatively at first, and then sliding his tongue across hers more hungrily as his kiss deepened.

Marina felt dizziness turning her as Lamar's kiss began to warm her. His hands moved from her face down to her shoulders, his fingers clutching her to him. She found herself kissing him in return, remembering how they had once been, and finding familiarity in him, in his touch and in his need for her.

She knew this man; he had been her best friend, he had been her lover. He had been the one she was going to spend the rest of her life with and even though he had hurt her tremendously, she felt all the time and pain between them dissolve like sugar in hot water, and it began to feel like the only love she had ever known.

His hands canvassed her back, rubbing her gently and touching all the places he used to touch. She closed her eyes, and it was like she was a teenager again. The scent of his skin was strange and yet familiar, it had a soothing effect on her. She used to lie in his arms, her body resting with his, and breathe him in. She was drifting through memories and thoughts of him as they grew closer and kissed deeper and longer. The feel of his skin against hers had been a comfort to her when they had been together, and now it was a familiar remembrance, like stepping back in time.

"Marina," he said, whispering her name as he kissed her. "My Marina." His mouth left hers and began to trail warm kisses down her neck. Her breath became shallow and she nuzzled his neck as his mouth covered her skin. She felt his hands move from her back down to her hips and he pulled her to him, pressing himself against her softly. It made her heart race and she gasped.

Something in her felt like it was rising up, as though she was in the depths of darkness where everything was slow and warm and she had to rise up to the surface to catch her breath. She opened her eyes as Lamar's fingers squeezed her hips and he began to move himself against her.

Her heart pounded and Kevin flashed across her mind. She felt anxiety replace all the warm electric current that had coursed through her and she placed her hands against Lamar's chest and pushed him. "Stop, Lamar, we can't do this," she whispered.

He leaned his head back and looked into her eyes. "Don't be afraid, baby, I'm not going to hurt you. I'm never going to hurt you again. All I want is to make you happy." He leaned back over and kissed her again as his hands continued to grasp her hips, pulling her to his stiffened groin.

Confusion had muddied her mind, but not her heart, and Kevin had hooked her and wasn't going anywhere. His face and his voice were lodged in her.

She turned away from Lamar and broke his hungry kiss. "Lamar, we can't do this. I'm not afraid to be close to you. It isn't that. This just isn't right, that's all."

He leaned back and looked at her again, his breath ragged, desire and need painting his face and filling his eyes. "Why isn't it right? We are both grown people who aren't tied down and I love you, Marina, I love you so much. Let's do this." He lowered his mouth to hers and kissed her again, adamantly, holding her tightly to him, but she pushed him away once more as it became clearer to her in her mind and heart that she wasn't doing what her heart truly wanted.

Her body was responding to him, her body was remembering all the passion and love they had shared, but her heart was not in the game, not all the way. Her heart was focused intently on someone else, and her heart wasn't going to let her get caught up with Lamar again.

"I can't do this because this isn't what I want. Can you understand that?" she asked seriously.

He looked carefully at her, realizing that she meant what she said. "Why not? What's holding you back, Marina?"

She stood still and silent for a moment, but then the words found their way to her lips and she breathed life into them. "I want someone else. I'm in love with someone else."

He took a step toward her and frustration crossed his face. "Who? The baby's father? Kevin? Is that who?"

She raised her chin. "Yes. Kevin."

Lamar closed his eyes and ran his hand over his face and then looked at her with guarded emotions. "Baby, you don't want to wait for him, he's already married. Don't do that. You know better than that. You have no business going after a married man! You have a daughter to think of, and you have your own future and your happiness to think of. I'm here, baby, and I want you. I love you, Marina, more than I ever did, and I want to be with you and help you raise that baby girl. I want to make a family with you!" He stepped closer to her and reached his arms out, closing his hands around her shoulders.

"Baby, I want you. I'm here. I'm available. I'm a viable option for you. He's not. He is married to another woman. How long have you known him? Almost a year now? From right before you got pregnant… and has he loved you all that time? You're going after something you can't have! Don't wish for that. Don't do that to yourself and Maddie. I'm here and I love you. I want to make a family with you for the rest of our lives. I'm your best option, baby." He made strong points, but she couldn't let go of what she wanted so much.

"He isn't going to be married much longer," she said quietly.

Lamar looked at her and blinked. "Why not?"

"He's going to leave his wife and get a divorce and then he's going to be with me and Maddie. He wants us."

He scoffed. "You sound like the other woman; like the mistress! Is that who you are? Is that who you want to be? You're better than that, Marina! You're worth more! You don't deserve to be someone else's mistress! You deserve a love of your own! Now! With me! Has he done anything to make that divorce happen?"

He had hit just the right chord with her. Nothing had happened. She looked down. "He needs more time. There are some legal problems that came up with his wife and he has to sort those out and then he can make his choice and come be with us."

"Make his choice? He hasn't even promised you yet that he will get a divorce? That he will leave his wife for you? What kind of man are you waiting for that feels like he needs to make a choice?

135

"There is no choice, there is you and there is the baby, and that's it! There's no choice! Do you know how many women out there have wasted years of their lives just waiting for a married man who said he would leave his wife for them? He's never going to do it! He's going to string you along like a lover, like a mistress, making you believe you mean something to him, making you believe that you have a future with him, and he will never live up to his word. He will never leave her and marry you.

"Don't you know that? Don't you know what you're getting yourself into here? Maddie needs a father who will be around her and help her grow up and you need a man who is committed to you, who loves you and wants you, and that's me! That's not some wealthy white dude who is already married! Come on, Marina, think about this!"

She thought about it. She knew it sounded sketchy, she knew it sounded trite, like so many other women who were sleeping with married men, men who promised them that they would leave their wives and start a life with their mistresses, but she believed Kevin. She knew he loved her, and she loved him so much and wanted a life with him so badly that she was willing to wait; she was willing to give him the time he asked for to make things work out so that they could be together.

"I have thought about it. He is what I want. He's worth the wait. He's Maddie's father, and she and I both deserve the chance to spend our lives with him. I'm not in any rush. I was going to have her by myself anyway. I hadn't planned on falling in love with him, and truth be told, I tried not to, but it happened. Having a man here was never part of my plan, but now if it happens, I want it to be him." She looked up into Lamar's eyes, and saw pain and need there.

"Baby, you loved me once. You could love me again, we could build a family, we could be happy! You shouldn't have to wait around! You don't have to wait around! Let me be here for you, let me be here with you! I love you! Doesn't that mean anything to you?"

She felt tears well up in her eyes. She covered her mouth with her hand and choked back a sob that was bubbling up inside her chest. Marina took a deep breath and then looked at Lamar again.

"I do love you, I always have, and it does mean a great deal to me that you are here and that you want us both, that you want to build a family with us. But you deserve to be loved like that in return, Lamar. You deserve a woman who wants you just as much as you want her. My heart is in someone else's hands right now. My love is all for him. I can't give you back what you want to give to me. I don't want to hurt you, but I do want you to understand clearly that you and I had our chance and we lost it. It's gone. I want him. I love him. I'm going to wait for him until he either makes up his mind to be here with the two of us or I fall out of love with him."

Lamar shook his head. "Don't do that. I can't stand to see you waste away waiting for someone who hasn't made you a priority in his life. I can't stand to see you used like that. You mean so much to me, you deserve so much better than that. Please, baby, please reconsider it and think about it. I'll wait for you, baby. I will, but you can't do that to yourself and Maddie."

She felt hot tears sliding down her face and Lamar, seeing them, pulled her to him and held her tight against his chest, rubbing her back. "Don't cry baby, please don't cry. I'm here. I'm here for you." He rubbed her back and soothed her until she was quiet and still, and then he looked down at her while she was in his arms.

"I'm still going to come around. I'm not going to stop seeing you just because you have your sights set on him. I won't miss any opportunity to be with you. I love you. I'm not giving up on you, not ever again." He leaned down and kissed her lightly and she let him, then he pulled her against his chest again.

She knew there was truth in what he said; many women were led to believe that they had a future with some married man when in reality, there would never be a future, but she just couldn't give up on Kevin. She fully understood Lamar's insistence not to give up on her in turn, and she could not deny him that opportunity.

"I understand," she said softly. "I don't mind if you come around, and I like visiting with you, but you have to know what the stakes are and where my heart really is. I don't want you thinking things that just aren't going to happen."

He rubbed her back again. "Alright. I'm going to be here. I'm going to be around so much that you'll change your mind. I will show you just how important you are to me, and then you'll choose the right man. Then you'll see just how good I am for you and Maddie, and you'll let go of that fool of a married man and live right." He kissed the top of her head, then reached his finger under her chin and tilted her face up to him, kissed her forehead softly, then her nose, and she smiled at him, and then he kissed her lips again, slowly, deeply, sensually, and her heart started to skip a beat.

She kissed him back for a moment; he moaned quietly and then held her face close to his and said, "You're going to be mine again. You are going to be my girl. I'm not giving up on you. You are going to be in my arms forever, baby. I lost you once already, but it's never going to happen again."

She tilted her head to the side and gave him an apologetic look, and then stepped around him and walked out of her bedroom and into the living room. He was close behind her. He hugged her goodbye and kissed her once more, lingering close to her lips and then he smiled at her and walked out the door. She closed it behind him and took a deep breath, pushing all the confusion from her mind.

When Kevin pulled up to the house and parked his car, he discovered that he wasn't alone on the street. He closed the car door and heard someone call him.

"Kevin," the man's voice said.

He turned, looking around him and saw Lamar standing across the road and a short distance away. Kevin recognized him as the man he had seen leaving Marina's once before, and he walked toward him with no expression.

138

"What can I do for you?" Kevin asked simply.

"We need to talk," Lamar said, grinding his teeth.

"Who are you?" Kevin asked, certain he already knew who the man was.

"I'm Lamar. I was Marina's fiancé," he said quietly. "Go for a walk with me. We need to have a conversation." He wasn't asking, he was requesting without another option.

Kevin looked back at Marina's house and then turned to face Lamar. "We can speak here."

Lamar shook his head. "I don't want Marina to see us talking. Let's walk."

Kevin sighed deeply and nodded his head. "Alright. Let's walk."

They turned together and walked near each other down the street until they rounded the corner and neither one said a word until they reached the park where Lamar spent the afternoon with Marina.

They sat on a park bench and Lamar started the conversation. "I know Maddie is your child biologically, but I also know you're a married man and, for some reason, Marina seems to have feelings for you. She seems to think that if she waits around for you that someday you might leave your wife and go be with her. We both know you're never going to do that. It's totally unfair of you to give her any kind of hope that you might ever be with her. I want you to leave her alone and tell her you aren't going to leave your wife. Be honest with her."

Kevin sat up straight and looked right at him. "I don't actually know what I'm going to do, and whatever happens, it isn't your business anyway."

Lamar breathed deeply and let the breath out slowly. "It is my business because I love her and I want to be with her, but she's stuck on you. You are holding her back from having a happy life. You're holding her back from being with me and having a healthy and loving relationship with a man who actually wants to be with her! You're being completely selfish!"

Kevin's voice grew sharp. "*I'm* the one who is being selfish? You left her at the altar! She said she would spend the rest of her life with you! You had her and you left her! How am I the selfish one?"

"You're married! You are married and you are having children outside of your marriage and hustling an innocent beautiful young woman with false hopes of love and a relationship! She is sitting there alone in her house with that baby girl waiting for you, believing your lies that you're going to leave your wife for her! You are using up every one of the days that passes that you aren't truly with her!

"That's her life, it's her time, every single day, and she is burning every one of them waiting on you to stay true to your word and leave your wife and go to her and the baby, and you aren't doing it! Every day you are still with your wife is another day of Marina's that you have used her, lied to her, let her believe she was important enough to you that each day might be the day that you actually put her first and leave your wife for her, and each night she goes to bed a loser. Each day she goes to bed sad and alone because you aren't there with her.

"Each day you have let her down and each night you go to sleep at your own home with your wife and you leave her hurt a little bit more, you leave her alone, and she doesn't have to be. She could be with me. She could be loved, cared for, happy, and fulfilled, but you won't let her have that because you are a selfish son-of-a-bitch who is putting his own desires above everyone else's interests." Lamar laid into him with scathing comments and an angry tone.

Kevin stood up and faced him, looking down at him with narrowed eyes. "You have no idea what you are talking about. You have no idea the sacrifices that I have made or the reality of what is going on in my life or in my home. You have no concept of the love between Marina and I and you dare to call me selfish! You left her when she believed in you the most; you walked out on her when you had a chance to be with her as her husband for the rest of her life!

"If you had kept to your word, she would never have had Maddie and she wouldn't be alone right now. You would be in her home, in her arms, in her bed with her every night and none of us would ever have even met, but you didn't put her first, you put yourself first. You gave your word to her and you broke it. You broke your promise to her before it was even made! You left her and hurt her more deeply than anyone ever has!

"It's no surprise to me that she hasn't taken you back yet. You think I'm being selfish? I wouldn't even be standing here in front of you if you had kept your word. I'll tell you something, Lamar, there is nothing so sacred as a man's word, and if you understood even a fraction of that concept, you would know why I have to do what I am doing to get out of my marriage so that I can commit myself fully to Marina. I have every intention of being part of her life in one way or another all the days of our life because we have a child together, and I will always take care of her and love her. She will have everything she needs!" His voice was raised a bit louder than indoor level.

Lamar stood up and looked Kevin directly in the eye. "Maybe she'll have the money she needs, but will she have the love? Will she have the companionship she needs? She may have said that she wanted to have that baby on her own and raise Maddie alone, but you don't know Marina like I do. You have no idea how hard it will be for her to be alone, especially if she is waiting around for you to decide whether or not you want her more than your wife."

Kevin glared at Lamar. "Does she even love you? Does she want you? Has she said it? I doubt it. She is a one-man woman and she wants me. She loves me! She doesn't want you, so going after her is nothing more than you pushing her to do something she doesn't want to do. She has no interest in you, Lamar! She wants nothing to do with you romantically! You burned that bridge when you left her! Trying to twist the branch of friendship that she has so generously extended to you into something romantic is not only unfair but also underhanded of you!

"She doesn't want you, Lamar. Respect that and let her go! Let her live her own life! You had your chance and you screwed it up. You lost it and you lost her. Leave like a man with some dignity!"

Lamar shook his head. "No way; I'm not leaving. I have another chance with her. I have another opportunity to make her mine. She gave me that chance when she let me back in her life, and she even let me kiss her tonight. I'm going to get her back and you aren't going to be able to stop me, married man. Why don't you just go home to your wife and leave that poor girl alone! Let her find some real love with someone who does love her!"

Kevin clenched his jaw. "Lamar, I'm going to tell you this right now. Back off Marina. Leave her alone and stay away from my daughter. She thinks that the two of you are friends, and I know you have more on your mind. You stay away from the house altogether. I don't want you around either one of them. You are finished there."

Lamar smirked and shook his head. "Oh no… no. I'm not ever going to give up on her again. I lost her once because I was a fool, but you aren't looking at a fool right now. I've learned my lesson. I know how amazing she is. I'm not going anywhere. I'm going to go after her even more than I already have been.

"I'm going to make that woman mine and I'm going to be there for her daughter every single day and raise her like she was my own, because Maddie needs a father around her all the time and Marina needs a man to love her every night and be with her every day, and that man is me.

"I'm not going to stop until she is my wife. Nothing you say is going to stop me from doing that. You've met your match, Kevin, and you are going to lose. Marina is going to be mine."

With that, he turned and walked away, leaving Kevin looking after him.

Kevin knew he was going to have a battle on his hands. He stood there watching Lamar walk away and then he sat quietly on the bench beside him. Lamar's words had pierced a secret truth he had been struggling with in his heart. He did feel as though he was stringing Marina along. He was a married man, he was living with his wife every day, although they only had a sham of a marriage and there was no love. She was pregnant and he had no idea if he would ever be with Marina.

Lamar was right; every night she went to bed without him. She was lonely, she was sad, she wanted him to be there. She had said as much to him since she had admitted her love to him, and the most he could do was say it back to her.

 He hadn't made love to her. He hadn't been there to comfort and care for her in person, but Lamar had been there… Lamar had kissed her that very day, he said. Kevin closed his eyes trying to block the imagined image of Lamar kissing Marina. He began to wonder how much of Lamar's words were right. He began to wonder if he was indeed being selfish; asking Marina to wait for him, asking her to hold her love back and wait in loneliness until he knew what he was doing with his life and his marriage. How could he do that to her?

He wondered what would happen if he let her choose… if he told her that she was free to be with anyone she wanted. What if he told her that Ellen was pregnant? Would she wait for him then? Would she be angry with him and let him go? Would her love turn to anger? Would she go to Lamar for comfort and love? Was it really selfish of him to try to keep her for himself?

A blizzard of questions confused him, raging through his mind. He sat on the bench for a long while, considering all of them. He didn't want a competition with Lamar. He didn't want to make Marina into some prize to be battled over and won like a trophy. He wanted to be with her because they were in love, because they wanted each other for the rest of their lives, not because he had bested another man for her heart and her future.

Kevin sat on the bench with all of those questions and many more racing through his mind, and a heavy heart weighing him down. He felt as though he needed some time to think through everything. He walked back to his car, got into it and drove away, and he didn't see Lamar watching him with some satisfaction when he left.

He headed back to his own house and he called Marina as he drove away.

"Hello, Marina," he said, so glad to hear her voice, but feeling quite low.

"Hi, I thought you would have been here by now, is everything alright?"

"Actually, there's been a little bit of a development on this end and I won't be able to come visit tonight. I'm very sorry, I really wanted to see you both, but I have some things to take care of that can't wait. Are you alright?" he asked, hopeful that she would be forgiving.

She was. "That's alright." She said after a quiet moment. "It's fine. I'll have dinner here."

"How is Maddie?" he asked, sorry that he hadn't seen her.

"She's fine. She's looking around at everything." There was a sadness in her voice and he knew that she was hurting.

"I'll see you soon. I promise. My word to you. I will be there as soon as I am able to be there." He hoped it would soothe her some.

"Alright. Take care, Kevin. I love you." she spoke softly.

"I love you too, Marina. So much." He hung up and sighed in frustration. He dialed the phone again and this time Jacob answered.

"How are things going, Kevin?" he asked curiously.

"They have certainly been better. I had a run in with Marina's ex-fiancé Lamar tonight. He wants to be with her and he's giving me a run for my money… or rather, for my lady."

Jacob laughed. "He can't be serious. He left her at the altar, didn't he?"

"He did," Kevin answered with a sigh.

"There's no way she's going to take him back. No woman gets over that kind of humiliation and pain. Not to worry too much about him. Let's focus on getting your situation figured out. How's the old ball and chain doing?" Jacob couldn't stand Ellen and he had a long list of unflattering pet names for her.

"She's extremely grouchy, slightly sick and her appetite for extra-marital trysts has increased. I am almost used to walking in on her mid-coital dalliances these days. I warned her that the baby is at risk, but she has no concerns for that, though she says the baby is the most important thing to her, if for no other reason than for the wealth that will come with it." He was thoroughly disgusted with her.

Jacob whistled through his teeth. "She sure is a piece of work. Are all the cameras still up at the house?"

"Yes. I've stopped looking at the feeds, though. There's only so much I can stand, and watching what amounts to sex tapes starring my wife and half the hired help around the house is more than I can reasonably stomach." Kevin's face turned in distaste.

"Well, you don't have to watch them, but you do have to keep them. I'll be over to collect more of them tomorrow. I'm going to bring an obstetrician over to do a blood test that will determine paternity of the child she's carrying. She's far enough along now that we should get a clean test out of her to find out what's really going on." Jacob sounded very sure of himself. "I'm sorry to say it, buddy, but I can't imagine that the kid she's carrying is really yours."

"Jacob, the pregnancy confirmation documents she has say without a shadow of a doubt that she got pregnant while we were in Hawaii. It's the only time I've slept with her in over a year. That might very well be my child; in fact, I would be shocked if it wasn't."

Kevin remembered the night they made love in the house on the beach in Hawaii and he had called out Marina's name as he reached his orgasm. He had wished so much that it was Marina rather than Ellen that he was with that night, and now she was pregnant and it was the only reason he wasn't with Marina. Irony abounded.

"Well, regardless, we are going to get the doctor over tomorrow and get this figured out once and for all. If that isn't your child, I will have divorce papers ready to go, and if it is, then I have some other options for her that may get you the divorce plus the child. I'll be over around noon. Please make sure she's around and don't tell her we are doing this, just let her know that we need to see her in your office after lunch. Can you do that for me, Kevin?" Jacob sounded hopeful and a bit happy in a self-satisfied way.

"Yeah, I'll have her there. Thanks, Jacob." He hung up and parked at his house, heading up to his room to bury his aching head in the deep pillows he hoped would block out all the chaos in his mind.

Chapter 9

When Kevin awoke the next morning, it was early and he found that he was fired with a blazing determination to make it a life-defining day. He knew that it would be the day that decided his future, and the future of the two women who were simultaneously central figures in his life. He showered and dressed, sliding his tie closed. He was always in a suit and tie, always dressed very well, and was often complimented on his style and class.

He went down the hall to Ellen's bedroom and knocked on her door. There was no answer. He knocked again and still there was silence. After waiting a few moments, he tried the door handle, but it was locked. He went down to the kitchen and found Sarah, his housekeeper.

"Sarah, do you have a key to Ellen's bedroom door, please?" he asked with a slight blush.

Her eyes narrowed and she tried to disguise the distaste in her expression, but she could not fully keep it from him. "Yes, sir, I do have a key. I'll get it for you."

He followed her to the pantry and she opened a sliding door in the wall that revealed rows of keys for different areas in the house as well as the other buildings on his property. She handed him the key and as she pressed it into his hand she said, "Sir, I don't know if you want to go walking in there first thing in the morning. You might find an unpleasant surprise."

Kevin pursed his lips and looked away, then looked back at her. "I understand, Sarah. Thank you for your concern. As always, your dedication and care is much appreciated." He gave her a smile and headed back up the stairs. The key worked and he pushed the door open.

Her room was dark. The curtains were drawn and no light filtered in through them. He walked over to them and pressed the button to open them. The electronic blinds slid open and wide brilliant shafts of light flooded the room. He shielded his eyes for a moment as they adjusted to the sunlight and then he turned toward her bed.

She was stretched across her enormous bed, lying across one man's chest, his arms wrapped around her, clutching one of her bare breasts, while another man was sleeping with his face between her thighs, resting on one of them with his arms wrapped around her legs. The three of them were completely nude. It was obvious that she had been entertaining both of them throughout the night. The light did nothing to wake them.

 Kevin walked over to the bed, sickened at the sight of the woman he had once loved so deeply and had wanted to spend his life with, and he wondered how all of that had been so keenly changed. It was as though his marriage to her and his life were a geological formation that had been sculpted and changed over time, the difference at first nearly undetectable, but now it was great.

He cleared his throat. "Good morning, Ellen." His voice was loud and firm in an effort to raise her from her slumber. Her long dark hair was splayed over the man's chest and as she turned her head slowly and opened her big dark eyes to look at him, the glossy locks shifted, catching the morning light and glowing golden brown. He hated that she looked so beautiful on the outside and used that beauty to hide a cunning and cruel heart on the inside.

She blinked up at him. "What in the hell are you doing in here? You have no right to be in this room!" she snapped at him and glared.

He looked at her without expression or emotion, masking everything raging through his heart and mind without even a single ripple on his serene exterior. "I have a right to be in any place in this house. I own it."

He slid his hands into his pockets and consciously stopped himself from clenching his fists. "I came to let you know that you need to come down to my office at noon. You have an appointment with

Jacob and I, and it's quite important. This will be one that you don't want to miss."

She sat up part way, leaning on the torso of the man she had been sleeping on and he stirred and opened his eyes.

"What the hell are you two doing now? What are you up to?" she asked with enormous suspicion.

The young man opened his eyes widely and gaped at Kevin. "Who is that?" he asked sleepily. "Are we going to add a third guy to the party?" he queried, sliding his hand down Ellen's back and over her hip, massaging her ass.

Kevin did not take his eyes off his wife. "Be there at noon. This is not an optional meeting."

Her glare transformed and her Cheshire cat smile spread over her face as she reached her hand to the man's crotch and began to run her fingers over him, stimulating him and making him erect. "I have guests, Kevin. I have previous obligations. I might be too busy with my friends to make it down."

Kevin wanted to turn away from her, but he felt like he would be conceding defeat if he did; like somehow it would be letting her win, letting her have the upper hand, and he simply could not let her think she had gotten to him. There was a pit in his stomach that was growing quickly, but he kept a stoic expression on his face.

The man Ellen was manipulating moaned and smiled, his hand reaching up to massage her large breast. She smirked at Kevin and leaned over to the man's crotch, opening her red lips and sliding her tongue out to run it over the tip of the man's erection. Her eyes stayed on her husband as if to spite him, to taunt him with pain and frustration.

He kept himself in check and said, "Ellen, be there at noon. Your financial future depends entirely on it. Have some class. You are acting like a hooker."

He turned his head away and focused on walking out of the door. Before he got to it, he heard the man lying beneath her say, "Who is that guy?"

"Oh, he's no one important," she replied to him, "he's just the money."

Kevin closed the door behind him and covered his face with his hands. He couldn't begin to imagine how their lives had changed so much that this would almost be the norm for them; that there would be so little love, so little caring, and absolutely no respect from her toward him.

He had stayed true to her, true to their marriage and his commitment to love and honor her all of her life. But it had turned into a nightmare, and he could not look back at their time together and find any memory, any time, when he could pinpoint the turning page that brought them to where they found themselves at present.

He realized that perhaps that was because she had been hiding her true colors and had finally begun to allow them to show. She was certainly no woman that he wanted to remain with in a marriage. He thought of Marina and her simple sweetness and beauty; her goodness and her kind and loving heart. He would count himself as the luckiest man in the world to be with her.

Kevin spent the morning in his office working, and at eleven o'clock, Jacob arrived with the obstetrician. "Good morning, Kevin!" He grinned at his friend and hugged him tightly. "Today is the day, buddy. Today we change your whole life. I've had it with that bitch. Today she goes down in flames."

"We don't know that," Kevin said solemnly.

Jacob looked at him carefully and tilted his head. "What's got you looking like that? What happened? I expected you to be a little brighter today."

Kevin leaned back in his chair and rubbed his fingers over his forehead, trying to push the morning's memories away. He closed his eyes. "Oh, I had to wake Ellen up this morning and she wasn't alone."

Jacob did not look surprised, but he did let a scoffing laugh go. "Really? Who else was with her?"

"Two men I haven't seen before. As far as I know, they don't work here, which is a change. Did you hire anyone new?" Kevin asked, realizing that it was a possibility they might be working for him and he just wasn't aware of it.

"No. She must have no end of opportunities to find friends, though," Jacob said, speaking only part of his thoughts. "Kevin, this is Dr. Branson. He's going to administer the paternity test today. We are doing it in the guise of a wellness check on the baby; testing for Down Syndrome and things like that. We are going to tell her that we just want to make sure the baby is strong and healthy and that if she doesn't get the test, she is out her monetary allowance until after the baby is born. That ought to get her attention and cooperation." Jacob was obviously enjoying the entire thing far too much.

"Pleased to meet you, Doctor, I'm sorry you had to come do this, and I apologize in advance if my wife is out of hand at all." Kevin had no idea how she would react to this meeting and to the testing he was going to submit her to, but he thought a warning and early apology was most likely in order.

The doctor smiled and shook his hand. "No problem. Jacob has explained some of your situation to me, and I am very glad to help you out with the testing. I think it's of the utmost importance that we determine the true identity of the father of the child she is carrying, as I am sure that may have quite a significant impact on your life."

Kevin almost rolled his eyes. "You have no idea, doctor. Thank you for doing it."

They got set up and the doctor took a blood draw from Kevin and then tucked it away. They were all three sitting together with refreshments when Ellen finally strolled into the office at half past noon. They looked up at her and only the doctor stood when she entered the room.

Kevin was relieved to see that she was dressed nicely and that she was neat and clean. He nodded at her. "Ellen, this is Dr. Branson, he's here to do some standard blood work for the baby. You'll need to listen to him and do whatever he requires you to do."

She smiled at the doctor, a sweet, charming, demure smile, one that belied her true nature and made Kevin look away from her in utter disgust.

She took the doctor's hand in hers and squeezed it warmly, holding it for a long and lingering moment. "I'm so pleased to meet you doctor. Thank you for standing when I came in. It's rare to find a true gentleman these days, and I can see that you are unquestionably a real gentleman." She gazed into his eyes and gave him her sweetest smile.

The doctor looked at her intently for a moment, letting her hold his hand until she wanted to release it.

She let it go and raised her hands to the low neckline of her button down dress, opening the first button and pulling the material apart enough that it gave the doctor a generous view of her ample bosom. "Do you want me to undress, doctor?" she said with an innocently poised seduction, watching him with her wide eyes.

He looked at her directly and shook his head. "No, ma'am, you may keep your clothes on for this appointment. I only need a vein." She smiled and slowly buttoned her dress back up as Jacob shot Kevin a loaded look.

The doctor helped her sit on the sofa and he prepared her for a blood withdrawal while all three men were silent.

"It's so nice to see a fresh face, doctor, my husband feels quite strongly about keeping me in the house and I don't get to see many people. It can be extremely… lonely…" she said softly with obvious meaning, looking up at the doctor and pushing her red lips out into a pout.

"Well," the doctor smiled down at her, "soon enough you will have your child and you won't be lonely any longer." He patted her shoulder and continued his blood draw. She looked dejected and chose to cast her eyes around the room rather than look at Kevin, who was watching her, and Jacob, who was shooting daggers at her with his eyes.

When the doctor completed his initial work, he turned and looked at the men. "This will be a moment, while I complete the lab work here, perhaps everyone might like a break?" he asked.

Jacob looked sharply at Ellen, who moved as though she was going to get up and leave. "Oh no, no, we are all staying here and awaiting the results. These are very important tests and we want to be sure that the baby is fine. Let's have lunch; we can all stay here and eat together and wait for the outcome of the tests."

Kevin put his hand over his mouth to hide the smile that wanted to grow there. He truly appreciated Jacob and his dedication. He called Sarah and had her bring lunch into his office for all of them. They ate in moderate silence as no one wanted to speak about what was really going on in their minds and the doctor was working while he was eating.

After a long while, and just about the time that Ellen was becoming highly annoyed and agitated, the doctor paused over his work and looked up, pursing his lips and blinking, then he walked over to Kevin's desk.

"These are the results of the tests I ran today," he said simply, placing a sheet of paper on Kevin's desk, and then looking up at the three of them. Kevin looked down at it and his face paled slightly as he looked up at Jacob who was watching him like a hawk.

The doctor took his glasses off and wiped them with a soft cloth, then placed them back on his nose and spoke softly. "The child that you are carrying, Miss Ellen, has no biological connection to Kevin's DNA whatsoever. There is no question that he is not the father of your baby."

Jacob whooped, he could not hold it in, and Ellen gasped, her jaw dropping wide open as she stared at all of them. Fury colored her face and she screamed before she could speak, like a hot teakettle on the fire that whistles before water is poured from it. Water poured from her angry eyes as she jumped to her feet and pointed her sharp red fingernails at Jacob and Kevin.

"YOU! You planned this! This is a trick! This is Kevin's baby! My doctor said so! He said I got pregnant while I was in Hawaii with Kevin! How dare you try to discredit me like this? It's a ridiculous plot!" she shrieked.

The doctor looked at her and shook his head. "Miss Ellen, there can be no mistake. It's a blood test and the DNA does not match. There is no way that he is the father. I ran it twice to be sure, but once was really all we needed. Some other man is the father of the baby you are carrying. I assure you that it is no trick or plot."

Jacob shook the doctor's hand with a huge grin on his face. "Thank you so much, good sir! You've changed Kevin's life for the better. You have no idea the good that you have done today and the many lives you have just improved. We're all grateful."

"I'm not grateful!" Ellen screamed, tears pouring down her face.

The doctor stared at her, horrified by her behavior, and moved to pack up his materials.

"Thank you for lunch. I'll mail you all the documentation for this when I get the report written up for her medical charts, and I will send a copy of the paternity test to her physician as well so her records are complete," the doctor said, somewhat uncomfortably. He walked out of the office and Sarah showed him to the front door.

Jacob nearly pounced on Ellen. "*You*... you are finished here, woman." He reached for his briefcase and pulled out several thick packets of documents.

He set them on the table and pulled two pens from his pockets. "Kevin, I'll want you over here with me," he stated with happiness and excitement. Then he looked at Ellen.

"Perhaps you'll remember this. It's the prenuptial agreement that you signed before you married Kevin. In this agreement, you promised that you would never have extra-marital affairs and that if you did, you would forgo any monetary gain from the marriage in the event of a divorce following said action on your part."

She glowered at him. "What does that mean?" she asked in a growl.

"It means, my dear, that because you cheated on your husband, and remember that we have substantial evidence of that, that you don't get one red cent from your husband when this divorce is finalized. You get nothing. No cars, no house, no alimony, no child support, no benefit whatsoever. Nothing but whatever you brought with you when you moved in. I think though, that Kevin will let you take your clothes and personal effects. You may not keep the jewelry, however, or the Lamborghini. Those stay with Kevin."

She turned bright red and screamed at him again. "How could you do this to me? I'm your wife! I'm pregnant! What do you think you're going to do? Throw me out into the street?"

Kevin rounded his desk and sat beside Jacob. "No, I am not throwing you out onto the street. I've purchased a little condo for you to live in. It's paid for. You will have a little sedan to drive around. I've set up a bank account for you in your maiden name and it has been funded with enough money to see you through for about five years if you live modestly. I feel that I owe you no more than that. In fact, I don't even think I owe you that, but I don't want to leave you with nothing."

She gasped and covered her mouth in shock and horror at the growing reality of what her life was about to become.

Jacob grinned. "Now that I've reminded you of this prenuptial agreement, you understand that there is no legal recourse for you; it would do you no good to try to take Kevin to court because you are already bound by the contract you signed before you married him."

Having said that, he reached over to the table and picked up a thin stack of pages that were stapled together, "I'm going to have you sign this divorce. It gives you back your maiden name and that is basically it. The divorce will be official as soon as the judge signs this. You will be moving out of this house today and into your new condo. I've arranged for a moving crew to come by this afternoon and help you get packed. I can't imagine it would take long, since all you are taking with you are your clothes and personal belongings."

She shook her head, her hand over her mouth, tears streaming down her face. Then she looked up at Kevin and shrieked at him. "You bastard! You absolutely rotten bastard! How could you do this to me?" she raged in fury.

He looked at her, watching her with a detached sort of emotion, and realized that the pain in him, the pain that had been there building up for so long, even the pain from seeing her with the two men in her bed that very morning, was dissipating, and in its place was a growing light and warmth. He was going to be free of her, and he would be able to be with Marina. There would be no guilt. There would be no conflict or confusion. He was going to be free.

"Ellen, you did this to yourself, and you did it to me. You chose every action and inaction you did. I stayed with you through thick and thin, and gave you the benefit of the doubt and I didn't even turn my back on you when I found out you were seeking lovers outside of our marriage. I was with you through all of it, and now it's time to cut it and let it go.

"We both need to focus on a new life without each other. I'm so sorry it worked out like this for us. I really loved you, but everything that has led us to this moment has been because of you." He spoke solemnly and watched her as she tried to contain her anger.

Jacob just grinned. "Do you need a pen? I have several. Any color you like." He set one on the table in front of her and she grabbed it up and signed the divorce papers in each place that he indicated to her. When she was done, she snapped his pen in half and threw it back at him.

"Do you have any questions?" Jacob asked her, jovially.

She seethed at him. "Yes. Where the hell are all those sex tapes at that you two recorded of me?"

Jacob leaned back and folded his hands in his lap. "They are safely tucked away. You see, those are a resource. An ace in the hole, if you will. If you give Kevin any grief over the next five years, if you harass him, if you ask him for money, if you slander his name, if you try to sell your story to the press, there will be repercussions. If you speak his name to anyone or try to make any part of his life public, including the lives of his child Maddie or her mother Marina, then every single one of those sex tapes is going to go live all over the entire world.

"If, after five years, you have kept your mouth shut and you never speak a word about Kevin, Marina or Maddie, and you go on your way like a good girl, I will personally guarantee that every sex tape we have of you will go back into your possession and no copies will be kept. My word to you.

"See, this is another opportunity for you to do the right thing instead of screwing up, like you seem to keep doing every chance you get, and if I may offer you a little bit of free advice... don't screw this up."

He leaned closer to her over the table, holding her eyes with his in an icy stare. "You screw this up, and your life will become a whole new experience in levels of hell that you have never even dreamed of. I promise you that." Then he leaned back and grinned at her again.

Kevin and Jacob watched her as she rose up unsteadily and walked out of the office. Kevin stayed in his office, wishing to give her some privacy as she left their home. He didn't want to see the carnage that was the remnants of his marriage as it bled out the door and into the street. But Jacob hovered near, watching silently and making sure that she neither damaged nor took anything that he had not said she could have.

He was right. It didn't take her long to pack her things, and the moving company had her out of the home by nightfall. When the door closed behind her for the last time and the locksmith began his work installing new locks on every door in and around the house, Jacob walked back into Kevin's office and sat down with him, pulling an ancient bottle of scotch out of his thick briefcase.

"What's that?" Kevin asked, a smile touching the corner of his lips.

Jacob poured them both a glass and set the bottle on Kevin's desk. "It is the best way to wash out the old and welcome in the new. You and I are going to polish off this bottle tonight, and tomorrow, you are going to have the freedom to do anything you want with your life. Tomorrow, I will track that judge down and have him sign your divorce, and then my friend, you can marry Marina anytime you like. Maybe you could even start shopping for rings tomorrow, if you want to."

Kevin felt a tear roll down his face. "It's a bit overwhelming," he said quietly, looking into the scotch and then up into Jacob's face. "I could never have gotten through any of it without you, my friend. Thank you." He toasted Jacob, and together they drank their glasses and then slowly, as the hours passed, they worked their way through the whole bottle.

It was the end of an era and the beginning of a new life. It was closure and opportunity, and it was one of the most significant days of Kevin's life, just as he knew it would be when he woke up that morning.

Chapter 10

Marina had been out walking Maddie in her stroller and as she came up her sidewalk and into the gate of her front yard, she was surprised to see a thick carpet of red rose petals lining the walk. She followed the path of petals up the stairs and saw that there were several bouquets of red roses around her front door. She gasped, looking around in wonder at all of them, dumbstruck by what she was seeing. She entered her home and saw that the path led through her living room, which was filled with more bouquets of roses and the path continued down her hallway and into her bedroom.

She placed her sleeping daughter in her crib in the nursery and closed the door before walking slowly down the hallway. She saw bouquets lining the hallway and the scent of the roses washed over her and through her.

It was a powerful trigger for her, because the flowers at her almost-wedding were all red roses. She couldn't stand them after her failed wedding day, but now they were everywhere and their scent took her back to that time and made her heady with memories and sentiment.

Marina opened her bedroom door and found that her room was filled with huge bouquets covering every flat surface in her room, and the trail of rose petals ended on the middle of her bed. In the center of her bed, where the rose petal trail ended, there was a white box with a white bow on it.

She lost her breath and could not begin to comprehend what was going on. She raised her hand to her mouth and tears came to her eyes. She suspected that it was Kevin, but she was surprised when she felt hands close around her waist and she turned to see Lamar standing there smiling down at her.

She gasped and looked at him in shock. "How did you get in here? How did... where did all of this come from? What's going on?"

Confusion tumbled the words from her mouth and she wiped the tears from her face.

"I know how much you love roses," he said softly, reaching up and brushing some of her tears away with his fingertips.

She didn't have the heart to tell him that since he walked out on her on their wedding day, she had avoided red roses at all costs. The overwhelming presence of them in her home was seriously affecting her, but she said nothing. She just looked at him in amazement. "What's going on here? I… I don't understand!" she cried quietly, as huge emotions pulled and tugged at her in different directions.

He reached his hands up to her cheeks, kissing her forehead, then her nose, and finally, he pressed his lips to her mouth in a gentle kiss. "I wanted to show you how much I appreciate you, baby. I wanted to show you how much I love you." He kissed her again. "I love you more than anything in this world, and you need to understand that." He moved his hand to the front of her face and his thumb pulled lightly on her chin, opening her mouth as he kissed her so that his tongue could taste her.

Confusion flooded through her heart and mind and she seemed to be drowning in the thick scent of the roses; his closeness to her, his hands on her face, his kiss that moved over and into her mouth, stealing away all of her resistance and reasoning. His kiss deepened and she slowly began to kiss him back, tears on her cheeks, visions flashing through her mind of her wedding day, of her white dress and her beautiful bouquet, of her limitless hopes and dreams, and her wide open heart.

His hands moved from her face, trailing slowly down her neck to her blouse. His fingers moved deftly over the buttons and pushed the material aside, and she drew in her breath, sure that she should stop him, but finding herself intoxicated by the blossoms that invaded her senses, her memories, her mind and her heart. He slid her blouse off and let it fall to the floor, and then reached behind her and loosened her bra, sliding his hands up underneath the material to cup her breasts and fondle her stiffening nipples.

The warmth of his touch took her to countless nights when she had lain with him in the bed they shared, when he had touched every part of her body so tenderly, so carefully, when he had made love to her for the first time, and she gave herself to him in her transformation from girlhood to womanhood. The memories of so many passionate days and nights as they learned about love with each other, as they touched and tasted, kissed and explored one another came back to her, submerging her in emotion and saturating her senses with the past.

Lamar's kiss grew hungry and insistent. His hands and fingers molded over the roundness of her breasts and he moaned in need. In a single movement, he lifted her and set her on her bed, laying her against the thick pillows.

Something in her wanted to pull away, but he covered her with his mouth and his hands, tasting, touching, drawing heat to her skin from her core and stealing away her very breath. She slowly shook her head trying to clear away all the confusion and connection between what was happening and what had happened between them before.

"Wait..." she said with a thin voice.

He was kissing the top of her breast, moving his open mouth over the full curve of it, and he traced the tip of his tongue to her dark nipple. It was aroused and hard, and he flicked his tongue back and forth over it, drawing more heat from her, but she repeated her plea to him, "Wait..." she whispered. He lifted his head and his eyes to meet her worried gaze.

"What is it baby?" he asked, leaning up and kissing her lips gently, tasting her, sucking on her lower lip, kissing her deeper and hotter, and then looking at her.
"What are you doing? What are you doing to me? What is all this?" she asked, looking around her at her bed, covered in petals. He

grinned and picked up a handful of them, letting them fall from his fingers one by one onto her bare chest, and then rubbing his hand over them to press them against her skin.

"Just a little show of appreciation. Just a little love for you," he said with a quiet smile. He sat up and reached for the box sitting in a pile of red petals in the center of the bed. Lamar pulled his shirt off and lay down beside her as she looked at him in confusion.

"You know what I missed most about us?" he asked with a smile.

"What?" she replied, not sure she really wanted to know.

"I missed the feel of your skin against mine. I love the way your body feels when it's connected to mine. I want that back. I want you back, baby. You know that. I want you back more than anything in this world, and I'm not going to stop until I get you back."

He kissed her again, deeply, sensually, caressing her neck, her shoulders, her breasts and her hard nipples. Then he sat up and looked at her with a smile.

"It's better than it's ever been with us, baby. Can you feel the heat? Can you feel the passion? It's like we've both come back together at our very best and now we can have each other and enjoy each other forever." He leaned back down and kissed her mouth, sliding his hand up her leg and underneath her skirt. Her eyes flew open and her hands clamped on his shoulders as his fingers moved hungrily over her flesh.

"Wait, Lamar… this… this is too fast, this is too… wait!" she said again as his fingers reached her underwear and began to anxiously manipulate her body. He pushed past her panties and slid his fingertips into her, rubbing her lightly.

"You used to love for me to touch you, all over your body, do you remember?" he asked softly, kissing the side of her mouth. "You loved my hands on you. You loved me inside of you."

She turned her head away from him slightly. "I do remember that, but we aren't like that now… Lamar, what are you doing?"

He pulled his hand from her skirt and leaned up on his shoulder, reaching for the box again, after having set it further back on the bed when he picked it up earlier. He handed it to her and grinned at her, reaching his empty hand up to massage her breasts and play with her hard nipples.

"This is a special gift for you. It's a promise," he said as she looked at him suspiciously and pulled the ribbon apart. She lifted the lid, a nervous feeling beginning to spin inside of her, and she tilted the box to look into it.
There in the center of the box was a giant red rose bloom, and at its center was a diamond ring. She gasped and covered her mouth, dropping the box as the nervous feeling in her exploded.

"I want you to marry me," Lamar said, pulling the rose out and sliding the ring from the petals that surrounded it. He looked at her earnestly. "I made a mistake once before, but I know what I lost and I have you back now, and I'm not going to lose you again. I'm going to marry you and keep you with me as my wife all of my days. I love you, Marina, and I want you to marry me. Say yes. Be my wife, Marina. Let me make you happy always."

She felt tears stinging her eyes and her throat burned with a sob that she could not let loose. She gasped for a breath and he watched her closely.

"Lamar…" she couldn't begin to explain to him what was going through her at that moment. All the happiness she had once known with him, all the passion and pain, all the time it took to heal and recover from the devastation he had wreaked on her heart and her life. It was all flowing through her as he laid there with her, the ring in his hand and his face full of love and hope.

"I can't do this!" she whispered.

"Of course you can baby, it's so simple, all you have to do is say one little word. Say yes, and I will put this ring on your finger and I will make love to you right now as if we were never apart, not even for a day. I will make all of your life something special and beautiful," he said, smiling and completely convinced that he was about to make her life perfect.

She shook her head. "No, Lamar, I can't do this. I love Kevin. I want him. I'm waiting for him."

Lamar grew visibly frustrated but held it in check. "Baby, no. You can't wait around for a married man who does nothing but lie to you. Is he here? No. He's at his house, with his wife, and you are here with me. In your bed, in my arms, and I love you, I want you, I need you, Marina. Marry me. Let me make you happy! Let me show you real love!"

She tried to swallow the lump in her throat. He was speaking aloud the things that plagued her in her dreams at night and in thoughtful clear hours of the day, when she wished that Kevin could be with her, but she knew he was with his wife. She had told herself so many times not to fall in love with a married man, but there was just nothing for it. She had fallen in love with Kevin, and when she finally admitted it to him, he had told her that he loved her back.

He said he was making up his mind about what to do with his marriage and with her and she had told him that she would wait. She had said that she would give him time to work through all the complications that he was struggling to solve. She had meant what she said; she would wait for him. She wanted him. She loved him, and when she heard Lamar say the things that he did, it cut at her heart; reminding her that she might be playing the fool to the man she loved.

"Baby, come on, please…" Lamar said softly, running his finger down her cheek and then pulling her into his arms to kiss her firmly, hotly, and deeply. His arms slid tightly around her and he held his whole body against hers, reminding her of what she had once known with him. His desire was obvious in the erection he pressed against her through his pants, and he began to rub himself on her in firm rhythmic motions.

She felt the warm skin of his chest against hers and it was the most intimate and familiar feeling she had with him since he had come back into her life. It took her back to their last days together, and their last night together, the night before their wedding, the last night they had made love, when he promised to love her and care for her all of her life. The night before he hurt her worse than she had ever been hurt.

She remembered his vows and promises, his declarations of love as he caressed her, as he kissed her, tasted her flesh and moved within her when they made love. She remembered how she had thought that she was feeling the height of love, the fullness of being one with another person, and then the devastating crash of a shattered heart the very next day when he deserted her and left her completely alone, caged in empty promises and broken dreams.

She pushed her hands against his chest and he looked at her in consternation. "Baby… please!" he whispered, the length of his erection pressed hard and firm against her thigh. "I want you back. I want to marry you. I promise… this time it will be the best decision you ever made." He began to move against her again, and she knew he was trying to arouse her, but her heart was centered solely on Kevin and nothing Lamar did could change that.

 She pushed him off her and climbed up off the bed. "No, Lamar. Having Maddie was the best decision I ever made." She pulled her bra back on and lifted her blouse from the floor, slipping into it and buttoning it back up as she spoke. "You made love to me before. You made promises to me before. You hurt me so bad, Lamar; you could never imagine the pain you put me through that time. I thought I was going to die. It took me a long time to find happiness again, and I have never known as much happiness as I have with my little girl, except when her daddy is around us.

"I don't care if he's married. If he stays with his wife, then we will just be friends and I will find a way for that to be good enough, because she deserves the best. If he chooses me, then we will be together and I will be happy. You want me to be happy? That's what I want. Respect that and honor it, because you owe me that, at the very least, if nothing else, you owe me that."

She shook her head at him. "Get up off my bed and get these flowers cleaned out of my house. I haven't liked red roses ever since you left me."

Lamar sat up in surprise and stared at her. "Marina, no! Please! Think about what you are doing!" he pleaded with her.

She closed her eyes in frustration and then looked at him squarely. "I have thought about it! I have thought about it so much over the last few weeks, Lamar… how it would be if I let you back in. Could things work out? I know it might work out alright. I realize that you might actually mean it this time and that we could possibly have a real wedding where you show up and we trade rings and tie the knot.

"I've also given a lot of thought to whether or not I really want that, and I will tell you something; every time I've thought about it, I've realized that that isn't at all what I want.
Now get all these flowers and that ring and get it out of my home. This is my home, and it won't ever be yours. You can leave now."

She spoke truthfully without malice, and strongly, without hindrance or hesitation, and she knew in her heart that she meant it.

Lamar stood up from her bed silently and pulled his own shirt back on. Then he cleaned up all the rose petals and put them in trash bags, hauling them out to his car. He came back in and looked at all of the bouquets of roses.

"What am I going to do with those?" he asked.

"Take them to a hospital; they will pass them all out to their patients. Take them to a retirement home. Go brighten a stranger's day."

"Marina…" he whispered.

She looked right at him. "No. Take them out and if you ever come back here again, it better be as my friend and only as my friend."

Seeing that she meant it, he took a deep breath and let it out slowly, shaking his head. Then he gathered the bouquets, and after several trips, his car was completely full of them. She watched him place the last one in his vehicle, climb into the driver's seat and pull away. As he did, she expected her heart to hurt, but she found that there was an enormous sense of freedom in her, as though her future was wide open, and it was a powerful feeling; one that made her feel as though she could fly.

Chapter11

Marina answered her phone with an enormous smile. "Hello!"

Kevin grinned at hearing her voice. "Hello, beautiful. How are you and Maddie doing today?" he asked with more happiness in his voice than she had heard since she met him.

"We're wonderful." She smiled happily.

"I wonder if I might take you girls on an outing today," he said with his own grin.

Marina was delighted. "I'd love that!"

"Good. I have a surprise for you," he said clandestinely.

"Okay!" Marina didn't care what they did, as long as she got to see him. It had been a week since she had seen him, and she missed him terribly.

An hour later, she and Maddie were riding in his car with him. They pulled up to an enormous home that was fronted by a lush and well-manicured garden filled with hedges, trees, fountains and flowers. Marina looked at the house in amazement, but she said nothing. He parked the car and helped her out of it, then lifted his daughter from her car seat and together they walked into the front door of the massive home.

Marina stopped in the foyer and looked all around her, and then she looked at Kevin as realization spread over her face. "This is your home."

He smiled at her. "No, Marina. This is our home. My divorce was finalized and my ex-wife has moved out. This home now belongs to me and to you, if you want to live here with me."

She gasped and stared at it with new eyes. She could not believe what she was seeing or what she had heard him say. He slid his hand into hers and said softly, "Come with me, my love, let me show you around."

He walked her through all the various rooms and showed her each of them in turn, while Maddie looked at him and patted his face and laid her head on his chest. They toured the kitchen and he introduced her to Sarah, who liked her immediately.

"Marina, this is my housekeeper, Sarah. She runs the whole house, and I have no idea how she does it. I could never manage without her. Sarah, this is Marina, and this is my daughter, Maddie." He spoke proudly, and Sarah was shocked for a long full minute, but then she took Maddie in her arms and played with her, kissing her and cooing at her happily.

"Miss Marina, I am so glad to have you here and to meet you. If there's anything I can do for you at all, you just let me know. I'll take good care of you." Sarah grinned at them both and finally relinquished Maddie back to her father.
They saw his office and he showed her the beautiful view of the garden from the window. Marina loved all of it. Then he took her up the winding staircase and stopped at the room down the hall from his, the room that used to belong to Ellen. He grinned at Marina and she opened the door.

Inside was a bright room filled with light colors and decorated as the most beautiful, fun, fantastical nursery that she had ever seen. Stuffed animals filled the corners, a gorgeous crib was set up in against one wall, toys filled the toy box and books filled the small bookshelves. A wagon stood waiting beside a tricycle, and mobiles and kites hung near a hot air balloon with a teddy bear in it, drifting beneath the cloud painted ceiling.

Marina was elated with it. She clapped her hands and took Maddie from her father's arms, showing her all the fascinating things in the nursery. Kevin walked with them, helping to point out all the best surprises. Maddie was completely taken with her new room.

Kevin then walked Marina to the room at the end of the hall and when she went in, she was stunned at the beauty and grandeur in the design. It was an enormous space, built with marble, wood and ceramic tiles. She had never seen another bedroom so grand. He walked up beside her and slid his arms around her waist.

"This is all yours if you want it," he said softly, whispering into her ear.

She turned to look at him with tears in her eyes. "What I want is you."

"Well, luckily, I come with the house," he teased and then touched her cheek. "Come with me, there's a little more to show you." He took them outside and showed them the pool, the pool house, the tennis courts, the flower gardens, the vegetable garden, the European gardens, and the private beach.

When they reached the beach, they stood looking at the sun as it began to sink into the warm colors of the late afternoon sky. He knelt down before her and took her hand in his while Maddie watched him from her mother's other arm.

"Marina," he spoke humbly, "I will love you always, and I will give you, Maddie and any other children we have together the promise of a lifetime of love and happiness. Please do me the honor of becoming my partner for life, my wife. Marry me, Marina. Make a family with me."

She could not stop the tears that spilled over onto her cheeks as complete happiness filled her whole heart. "Yes, Kevin. I will marry you. I will spend the rest of my life with you. I love you," she said simply, with a huge smile on her beautiful face.

He rose, choked up with overwhelming emotion, and held her and his daughter in one big hug. Then he slid a stunning diamond ring on her left hand and kissed her cheek.

"Shall we put her down for the night?" he asked, looking at Maddie as she lay on her mother's shoulder with sleepy eyes.

They walked back to the house and put their daughter in her new nursery, and then Kevin took his fiancé to their room and closed the door behind them. She turned in a circle, staring at the enormous room around them, and then her gaze stopped on the handsome man in the suit and tie who was gazing at her, watching her with hungry eyes.

Her breath caught and he walked slowly toward her, enjoying every single moment of it. He reached her and took her hand, raising it to his mouth and kissing her fingertips lightly. Then he led her to the giant bed near the French doors that opened onto the balcony overlooking the gardens. She stood before him and he traced his fingertips slowly down her cheek.

"I've waited so long for this. I have wanted you more than you will ever know, and I will always want you this much and probably more. I need you." He lifted her chin and closed the distance between their faces until they were almost nose-to-nose, eyes closed, and she could feel his breath on her lips.

"Thank you for becoming my wife," he said softly, and then he pressed his lips to hers ever so gently, brushing them over her skin and learning her curves with his mouth and the tip of his tongue. She gasped as the butterflies in her went wild and heat flooded her core and careened through every part of her body.

She touched her dark fingertips to his suit and began to pull it from his body, one piece at a time until there was nothing between them but warm air. Their heartbeats grew faster and their breath grew shallow as desire burned hotly in them. She too had waited, just as long as he had, for this night, this time to be together, and they both were consumed with every passing moment, every touch, every taste, every kiss, as they explored one another slowly, achingly, and reveled in it.

Kevin looked at her body as though it was the first time he had ever seen a woman, and as he gazed upon her, he knew that he never wanted to see any other woman besides her for the rest of his days. His fingertips touched all of her curves and lines, felt the heat that emanated from her, and sent electricity into her body that she had never known before.

She felt every part of him, running her hands and fingers over his muscles and his flesh. He grew hard with need for her and he closed his eyes as her fingers closed around him and touched him, stimulating him, massaging him until he could not hold in the moans of desire that escaped him.

"I have wanted this for so long," she whispered, her breath short and ragged.

"As have I, my love. It has been the most difficult experience of my life to wait for you, to hope that someday I could love you like this, touch you, hold you and love you like I have wanted to. You bring me such happiness, but this is more than I ever imagined. I could not have dreamed you more beautiful than you are. You amaze me."

He lifted her up and laid her across his bed, sliding his hands over her body and caressing every part of it. "You are like nothing I have ever seen or touched," he spoke, his lips against her skin, his tongue tracing flames over her.

Marina thought she had known love and pleasure, but nothing in her life had ever prepared her for the ecstasy that saturated her when he traced his tongue up her inner thighs and lost himself for what seemed like ages in the exploration of the core of her body with his tongue and lips. She held his hands tightly and her soft cries became louder as he tasted her. Drinking her in, he brought her to a heated climax over and over again. When he could no longer hold himself back from her, he lifted himself above her, moved between her thighs and pushed his erection into the hot dark depths of her, burying himself in her body and in her love.

She wrapped her arms and legs around him tightly and together they moved as one, losing their own individualities until there was nothing left but togetherness. She clasped at him, holding him to her with every ounce of her strength as he filled her with himself, giving her pleasure beyond her imagination. Then, as they wrestled with passion growing faster and fiercer, he pulled her hips firmly to his and thrust himself as far into her as he could, emptying the fires of himself into her until they both collapsed in bliss and exhaustion.

Kevin finally caught his breath and looked at her. "Marina," he said softly as his heart began to slow. "I have never felt anything like you in my arms before. I know right now that I will never get enough of you. I will never know a day when I am not aching to be inside you, loving you," he leaned over to her and kissed her sensually on her full lips, "losing myself in you. Can you give me that?" he asked, looking into her blue-gray eyes.

"Yes, my love. Gladly." She slid her dark fingers over his back and pulled him to her body again. She lowered her mouth to his rising erection and with her tongue and lips, kissed him, swallowing him and sucking on him until he became completely aroused again, arcing his back and moving himself into and out of her mouth and throat until he could no longer stand his ache for her body.

He pulled himself from her hot mouth and laid her back on the bed, his hands reaching low and spreading her thighs apart, then rubbing himself against the outside of her body in her heat and moisture, making her gasp and hold tightly to him. He maneuvered against her core for only a few moments before he pushed the pulsing tip of himself into her.

There was no time to explore as they began to make love again; the urgency of their need was too great. They had tasted the best of each other, and both of them needed more of the same as though it was oxygen and they could not live without it.

He entered her swiftly in breathless need, moving in and out of her as slowly as he could, learning her body as they moved, holding her tightly to him, sucking at her breasts and teasing her nipples, clinging to her hips and pulling her snugly against his own, until before long, they were gasping in each other's arms again.

They finally fell asleep in utter happiness, awash in love and joy. When they woke, they made love, and then showered and tended to their child, and every chance they got, they found themselves in each other's arms, in each other's bodies, in each other' hearts.

In no time at all, the feel of the house changed, and it was filled with laughter and happiness, with love and great joy, as the members who lived in it made their family strong within the great walls.

A small wedding was held on the beach where Kevin had proposed to Marina, and their friends and a few family members congratulated them and wished them a lifetime of happiness, health and prosperity. It wasn't long after the wedding that Kevin and Marina announced that they would be adding a second child to their family, and they knew no greater joy.

Their happiness lasted all of their days as they finally welcomed five children over the years into their lives and home, raised them together and put the dark memories of their pasts in the shadows that the brilliant light of their love and lives created.

THE END

Did you enjoy this story? Please leave a rating on the store!

LEAVE MY REVIEW NOW!

ALSO BY CJ HOWARD

SEDUCED BY MR BIG STUFF

Harvey Mann has it all. Good looking, Wealthy, Intelligent and he can have any woman he wants.

Well almost any woman that is...

Stacey fails to see what other women see in him. She sees him as an arrogant player who is totally in love with himself. He is the type of man she was warned by her mother to stay away from.

However, fate eventually brings her and Harvey closer and Stacey begins to discover his more sensitive side which leads her into discovering exactly how Harvey got the nickname of "Mr Big Stuff"....

Is Stacey set to become yet another notch on Mr Big Stuff's bed post or is there something more to this relationship? Furthermore, has Mr Big Stuff finally met a woman who can actually challenge him?

Manufactured by Amazon.ca
Acheson, AB